The Physicians of VILNOC

A PENRIC & DESDEMONA NOVELLA IN THE WORLD OF THE FIVE GODS

Lois McMaster Bujold

SUBTERRANEAN PRESS 2021

The Physicians of Vilnoc Copyright © 2020
by Lois McMaster Bujold.
All rights reserved.

Dust jacket illustration Copyright © 2021 by Lauren Saint-Onge.
All rights reserved.

Interior design Copyright © 2021 by Desert Isle Design, LLC.
All rights reserved.

First Hardcover Edition

ISBN
978-1-64524-021-1

Subterranean Press
PO Box 190106
Burton, MI 48519

subterraneanpress.com

Manufactured in the United States of America

For all the practitioners through the long, long history of medicine who tried the wildest experiments, often failed, sometimes succeeded, and helped make our world.

"The gods have no hands in this world but ours.
If we fail Them, where then can They turn?"

—Ingrey kin Wolfcliff, *The Hallowed Hunt*

WITH FOUR PERSONS in three bodies competing for one infant, Penric mused, it was a wonder his new daughter Florina was ever allowed to touch her cradle. He tickled her cheek with one long, ink-stained finger, and smiled as she smacked her tender lips and turned her head.

"Give her over, Penric," said his mother-in-law, Idrene, genially. "Or is that Desdemona doing the doting?"

"It's me," said Penric. "Novice fathers are allowed to dote, too. And Des is actually only about two-twelfths baby-mad."

"True," put in his resident demon Desdemona, necessarily speaking through Pen's mouth as she shared his body—the sole way such a being of spirit could maintain itself in the world of matter. *Parasitical* was not the right term, as she gifted him with his powers as a Temple sorcerer in return. *Renter* was not just, either. *Rider and ridden* was the most common metaphor, with the implication that an out-of-control chaos demon could reverse the position of power if the rider-sorcerer was weak or careless. Penric usually settled on *person*, which was both conveniently vague, and had the bonus of gratifying Des.

Desdemona gossiped on, "Litikone and the physician Helvia were always the baby-fanciers among us. Amberein and Aulia preferred children able to talk. Ruchia and Mira were indifferent to the nursery set. And Rogaska disliked everyone equally, regardless of age." Not the full tally of ten women (and the lioness and the mare) whom Des had occupied and been imprinted by over the span of her two centuries in the world, but Idrene nodded understanding, while also taking the opportunity of Pen's distraction to swoop in and snitch the sleepy Florina from his grasp.

"I don't recall the old general as doting," Idrene remarked, securing her grandchild on her shoulder and patting her fondly. "More daunted, really. Which is odd, considering how fearless he was about army affairs. But then, like you and Nikys, he'd waited a long time for his firstborns."

"Thirty-three is not old," asserted Penric. Well, not for him. Maybe for first-time-mother Nikys who, after a childless prior marriage ending in a premature widowhood, had feared herself barren. "Nikys's papa was, what, fifty when she and Adelis were born?"

"Around that. There, there, little Florie," Idrene cooed as the infant stirred and daintily burped. "I'm glad you and Nikys gifted her with that name. My Florina would have been so honored."

Pen had been surprised to learn, upon his first acquaintance with Idrene, how cordial the much younger concubine's relationship with her husband's first wife had been, free of the bitter rivalry and jealousy reputed to be more common in such situations. Entirely to his benefit, as Nikys's upbringing in that household had possibly prepared his wife for the complexities of living with two-personed Penric. Idrene as well, come to think.

"I'll hold out for *Llewyn* next time," sighed Pen.

Idrene's dark eyes crinkled in amusement. Even on the high side of fifty, she was still a handsome woman, straight-backed, with warm dark copper Cedonian skin and black hair like her daughter, though her curls were salted with silver. "Next time, eh? I like the sound of that, but what if it's a boy? I can't always tell if those bewildering Wealdean names you favor are for boys, or girls, or both."

"My late princess-archdivine back in Martensbridge was a woman, but in fact that name could go to either sex. So I'm prepared regardless."

Through Penric's open study door, a knock echoed faintly from the street-side entry downstairs. He relaxed as he heard their housemaid Lin answering it.

Idrene, by contrast, raised her head with the perky alertness of a cat sighting a mouse. "Is that Adelis's voice?"

"Sounds like it," agreed Pen as a low rumble, too distant to make out the words, wafted up through the atrium. *Yes,* confirmed Des, whose demonic senses left her in even less doubt than Idrene's maternal ones.

"Oh, Nikys will want to know. Where is she?"

"Setting up her loom in her workroom." Which had been how he'd managed to capture Florina, briefly.

"I'll tell her," said Idrene, marching out still holding her prize. "You can go down."

"Adelis more likely came to see you two than me," Pen protested. But, abandoning the mess of correspondence on his writing table that he'd been ignoring in favor of his much more fascinating daughter, he rose amiably and went to descend the gallery stairs. The stone-paved atrium in this leased row house was scarcely wider than the hallways in the wooden houses of Pen's home country, but it served to let in light and air. And rain, which Pen had needed to grow used to, as it rather violated his notions of indoors versus outdoors. Snow, in the duchy of Orbas, was not a hazard.

The sturdy front door gave directly onto the street. Penric did not keep a porter to guard it, as the knowledge that the house belonged to a sorcerer was usually enough to buffer unwanted intrusion.

Lin ducked her head at him as he strode up. "Learned, General Arisaydia is here. But he refuses to come in!"

"Hm?" Pen poked his head out his doorway.

His brother-in-law, dressed in standard-issue tunic, trousers, and boots, but dispensing with his leather cuirass and the red cloak of his rank on this warm summer day, hovered at the base of the few steps gripping the reins of his horse. A younger man, aide or groom, stood holding the reins of two more, army-saddled likewise.

"Adelis, pray enter. Nikys and Idrene will be glad to see you. Your niece is awake, by the way."

Adelis made an unexpected averting gesture, and said, "No!"

"...What?"

"I mustn't come inside," Adelis went on, looking very determined about it. Adelis being capable of impressive stubbornness, Pen didn't argue.

"In a hurry, are you?"

"Yes. I need you to ride out to the fort and look at something. Now."

Pen blinked, taken aback at this vehemence. The post that the young general commanded for the duke of Orbas lay about a mile inland from the town of Vilnoc's own walls, up the valley and overlooking the main road west. It had once stood closer, Pen understood, centuries back when Orbas had been a province of the Cedonian Empire, and before the port had followed the slowly silting river mouth downstream. Duke Jurgo tried to maintain most of a legion there when at residence in his summer capital, although his main defensive interest lay on the harbor side with his navy. With several thousand men and camp followers, the fort was almost an outlying town in its own right.

Adelis would hardly be consulting Penric, with such urgency at that, on military affairs. This left something theological, unlikely; something to do with a translation problem, possible in light of his scholar's command of languages; or some suspected magical problem, usually mistaken but, rarely, real, and thus interesting. Or…

"A number of my men have contracted a strange fever."

Or that. Yes. Agh. "Don't you have army physicians for such? Experienced with camp dysentery and so on?"

"It's not that. Anyway, we keep our barracks and wells and latrines clean, and our rations fresh. My physicians can't identify it. A couple have come *down* with it, and some of the orderlies, too."

"You know I do not practice medicine," said Pen stiffly. "Anymore."

Adelis made a swipe of his fist, dismissing Pen's aversions. "Four men died last night. *More* men. Six in the previous few days."

Pen hesitated. "How long has this been going on?"

"Ten days for certain. How long before that, no one is quite sure. But it's recent, it's spreading, and it is much more lethal than dysentery."

"Who survives it?"

Adelis scowled. "It may be too early to tell."

That does not sound good, observed Des.

Truly. Any virulent disease that infected the fort was sure to jump to the port, and that included Pen's front door, and the human treasures behind it. Adelis standing well away from that same door told its own tale.

"I'll fetch my case," sighed Penric.

He returned upstairs to the bedchamber that he shared with Nikys and, now, Florina's cradle. The case containing the tools of his third, no, fourth trade—after learned divine, sorcerer, and scholar—rested in a chest out of sight and preferably out of mind, but should he want them at all, they were of finer make than army-issue. He shucked off the comfortable, threadbare old tunic he'd been sluffing about the house in this morning, and donned his second-best summer vestments for a divine of the Bastard's Order.

Slim tan trousers. Sleeveless cream tunic split at the hips falling to panels fore and aft his knees, hems decorated with a frieze of embroidered holy animals; secured by the sash at his waist with a silver cord in its braid denoting, or warning of, his calling as a sorcerer. He left the silver-plated torc for the tunic's high collar with his first-best togs, reserved for court ceremonies and holy days, in the chest.

He stuffed his old clothes, along with a change of smallclothes, into a sack. He hoped he wouldn't need to be gone overnight, or longer, but one never knew. He could borrow clean army garb from Adelis in a pinch, but any trousers would fall hopelessly short of his ankles.

Upon reflection, he wrapped his long blond queue in a knot at his nape, fastening it firmly. He didn't need it falling forward and trailing through the messes sick men leaked. He was just finishing this task when Nikys hurried in.

"Penric! What's going on?"

"Your brother wants to drag me out to his fort to see some of his men who've come down ill." Pen decided not to mention the death count.

"He knows better than to tax you with that sort of task." Her frown deepened. "Which means this is something out of the ordinary, doesn't it." Swift deduction, not question.

"Well, I won't find out till I—and Des—take a look at it. I'm rather counting on Des." Who had much longer experience than he did.

Entering his arms, Nikys took a deep breath, pleasantly ample to hold—Pen allowed himself a moment of covert appreciation. "Then I'll count on her as well." She laced her hands around his narrow waist in turn. "Don't let him get in over his head, Des."

"I'll do my best, love," said Des through Penric's mouth.

One of the many delights of his delightful wife was the ease she had developed in telling them apart, and she nodded without confusion. "How long will you two be gone?"

"Not sure," said Pen. "An hour, a day, a week? I may need to intern myself for a bit before I come back here."

"It's that contagious?" Her deep brown eyes widened, looking up at him in alarm.

"Mm, perhaps not for me. I didn't contract tertiary fever during my year in Adria, and it's endemic there. I haven't even caught a cold since I came to the Cedonian peninsula." Being knocked on the head and tossed into a bottle dungeon or suffering magical attack from that out-of-control Patos sorcerer did not count as diseases, and Des had healed him of those injuries, too. But Nikys, nursing, was indivisible from their infant daughter in terms of exposure to anything chancy. He was confident she'd share his caution.

"So don't fret if you don't hear from me. It just means Adelis is keeping me busy."

"Humph. Don't let him treat you like one of his army mules, or I'll have his ears."

He kissed away her sisterly scowl, following up with kisses to her elusive dimples—ah, there, much better—and reluctantly took his leave.

ADELIS KEPT them to a swift trot on the short ride, impeding conversation, just as well. He was a tactician, not a physician. His army medics would inform Pen of the messy details soon enough, in their mutual language of the healing arts.

Penric had only been out to the fort once before, for Duke Jurgo's ceremony honoring his new general upon his successful return from the campaign against the incurring Rusylli. Devised to impress the assembled troops, no doubt, but Pen suspected Adelis had been more gratified by his witnessing family, small though it was: Idrene and Nikys and, yes, Pen and Des.

The fort spread over a low hill, with much less elevation than the castle-crowned crags of Pen's home country, but then, the old Cedonian military engineers had always been keen to assure access to water in these hotter lands. They'd made up for it by digging a large fossa around the extensive perimeter, a ditch that had to be periodically cleared of silt, debris, and villagers trying to build right up to the walls.

They clopped across the drawbridge and through the main gate with its flanking stone towers. Inside, they dismounted and handed the horses off to the aide, who towed them away to the cavalry stables. The elite mounted troops and couriers lodged with their beloved beasts on this side of the fort, along with most of the workshops, the smithy, stores, and the armory, though the bulk of the remounts and draft animals were pastured down by the river. Adelis led Pen through to the open central space, more than courtyard, less than parade ground, used for mustering, returning salutes from a few soldiers along the way, a brief tap of the right fist to the chest.

As they strode past, Adelis spared a five-fold tally sign for the fort's temple, which faced his headquarters across the square. Pen, belatedly, copied him, waving his hand down forehead, mouth, navel, and groin, but spreading it properly over his heart, as this temple was dedicated to the Son of Autumn, god of comradeship and thus, alas, war. And then Pen's habitual extra tap of the back of his thumb to his lips, for his own god's ambiguous blessing.

The activity under the sacred portico suggested preparations for a funeral. Not unusual, given the population here, but still…

They angled around the rows of barracks to the back corner of the fort given over to its hospice. It had its own small gate leading to a colonnaded court, and just inside a shrine to the Mother of Summer, patroness, among other things, of healing. Rather the opposite of the aim of an army, Pen fancied, but he glimpsed what seemed to be an unusual number of supplicants perched on the prayer rugs spread out before Her shaded altar.

Treatment rooms, stores, an apothecary, and its own bathhouse and laundry ringed the sunny court. The quiet far side, under its colonnade, was lined with chambers for patients, each door in the row made—somewhat—private by a leather curtain. Four to ten cots per chamber, depending on demand, so the place, Pen had been told, could accommodate up to two hundred sick or injured men at a time.

Adelis went to one of the leather curtains and pushed through, Penric on his heels, and the bright serenity of the courtyard was abruptly replaced with a shadowy scene of turmoil.

His eyes adapted quickly enough without Des's proffered help, though the details were no reward. Six cots set up, all occupied, five by groaning, restless men, one by a figure gone too still. Kneeling at its side a young man bent weeping, his shoulders shaking as he choked his grief into silence.

"Oh, no," breathed Adelis, stopping short. "Not Master Orides. I'd hoped you could save him at least, Pen."

Pen suspected Adelis hoped for a lot more than that, and flinched in prospect.

Orides was the senior physician of the legion. Pen had met him but briefly at the campaign celebration last year, finding the officer level-headed as only years of experience could bestow, a trifle dyspeptic—

possibly also from the years of experience—but with a sly wit. The crow-visage jutting up from its pillow bore no humor now, humanity fled with life's warmth, the darkened flesh shrinking to its bones seeming prematurely mummified.

Des, Sight.

His demon lent him her spiritual perceptions only at Pen's request, because the dual vision could be overwhelming, and his reacting to things no one else could see alarmed those around him. Ghosts, for example, although when he'd last been out here the fort had not been more rife with sundered souls than any other building of like age. But Orides, it seemed, was already gone to his goddess, gathered up like the valued child he must have been to Her. The scent of that passing divinity was fading like a whisper of perfume. *That much grace, at least, in this graceless moment.*

The young man looked up at the sound of Adelis's voice and scrambled to his feet, visibly pulling himself together. He tapped his fist over his heart, and in a squeezed voice said, "Sir!"

There was this to be said for military garb; you could tell who a person was, or at least their function, at a glance. Temple robes likewise, Pen supposed. This one was a young medical officer, by his green sash and somewhat stained, sleeveless, undyed tunic. In his early twenties, perhaps? His coloration was typical of this region: dark coppery-brick skin, black hair, brown eyes; his build average, his height a little under Adelis's muscular middle stature. His drawn, exhausted face was not standard-issue, nor his heartbroken whisper: "You're too late."

Adelis flicked his gaze aside at Pen's wince and, perhaps wisely, elected to let this outburst pass unremarked. "Penric, this is Orides's senior apprentice, Master Rede Licata. Our second medical officer." First, now, apparently, and by Rede's indrawn breath he was just realizing the full burden that had fallen upon him. "Master Rede, this is Learned Penric kin Jurald, Duke Jurgo's Temple sorcerer. He and his demon, Madame Desdemona, have experience in medical matters, and I trust will be able to help us sort out this crisis."

Adelis did not, to Pen's relief, name him a physician outright. Though the general's touch to the burn scars marring the upper half of his face like red-and-white owl feathers, which framed eyes that could again *see out*, suggested he was tempted to.

Des just preened a trifle at the rare nicety of being separately introduced.

Only the continuing swipe of his hand through his hair betrayed how harassed Adelis was feeling. With a chin-duck toward the cot, he went on, "When did he pass?"

"Not half the turning of a glass ago." Staring down at his late mentor, Rede rubbed the back of his wrist over his reddened eyes, and finally thought to offer, "It was probably already too late by the time you rode into Vilnoc this morning."

Adelis hissed through his teeth. "I daresay."

The smell of death was a misnomer, and really didn't apply till a corpse was well along, but the stink of sickness here masked all else, despite the diligent efforts to keep the chamber clean. An orderly glanced up from holding a basin for another patient to weakly vomit into, and called to Rede, "I'll help you lay him out next, sir."

Rede waved him back to his task. "He'll wait for us now."

"That feels so strange. He was always hurrying us along."

"Aye," sighed Rede. He made to draw the stained sheet up over Orides's face.

Pen raised a stemming hand. "I had better take a close look at him."

"Oh. Yes." Rede grimaced. "I think he would actually appreciate that."

Adelis stood back, arms folded, face grim, as Pen, Rede looking over his shoulder, bent to examine this most notable victim of the mysterious malady. He folded the cover all the way down and studied the corpse systematically from the toes up, neglecting no part.

Alive, Orides's skin had been the color of some warm wood or spice. It was darkened all over now to a grayish sort of blotchy purple. No external eruptions or lesions, though his pulpy flesh had started to break down at the pressure points where he'd rested on the cot, the bedsores looking like ones developing for weeks, not days. Eyes, ears, nose, and the inside of his mouth were traced with drying blood but not otherwise markedly different from any other dead man's. No special tell-tale stenches. The sunken flesh was similar to the parched state of several common diseases that rendered persons unable to keep any fluids down.

Sight again, please.

His soul is taken up.

Yes. But give me everything material you can.

The room faded away, and the weird, familiar sense of descending like a disembodied eye into a miniature somatic world replaced it. So, the empurpling *was* bruising, of a sort; not from blows, but as if the tiny blood vessels had disintegrated from the inside out, leaking their contents to coagulate and darken. The effect was apparent all through the body, not just at the skin, including in the lungs and gut. Pen extracted his extended senses as though pulling himself out of a bog. The sense of sticky horrors clinging to his skin was illusory, he reminded himself firmly, though he wanted to wash his hands at his first chance.

Mindful of the sick men in the beds nearby, Pen lowered his voice. "The victims vomit, cough, and pass blood?"

"Toward the end, yes. It's the sign." Rede's mouth tightened. "Master Orides knew."

"Had he performed any autopsies on the earlier deaths?"

"Yes, the first two." Rede's glance also went to the wary eavesdroppers on the nearby cots. "If you've seen all you can, Learned, perhaps we should take this conversation to the courtyard."

"Ah. Yes."

Rede covered his master's body once more, and made the holy tally sign with an extra tap to his navel. They shuffled back out to the bright courtyard, Adelis himself holding the curtain aside and exiting with alacrity. He was a brave man, Pen thought, but this wasn't the sort of enemy he could face with a sword or spear, for all that it was killing his soldiers in front of his eyes.

Rede sank down on one of the stone benches under the colonnade, squinting through puffy eyelids. In this better light, he looked even more strained, and Pen wondered when he'd last slept. Probably not last night. Adelis leaned against the nearest pillar, head bent with the labor of listening hard—not to their low voices, but to what they conveyed.

"I suppose I should begin with the obvious questions," said Pen. "What is the course of this thing? How does it first present?"

Rede shrugged in frustration. "At first, it appears as a common fever, the sort that passes off on its own with a few days of rest. Headache, and pain in the joints and muscles, loss of appetite. After a day or two, stomach pains start, with loosened bowels, again nothing unusual. The first certain sign is tiny spots under the skin, hard to make out. Then the skin starts to bruise, the spots growing to blotches and coalescing, as you saw. Then bloody or darkened stools and labored breathing. The descent into death is swift after that, three days or less. Altogether, from four days to a week."

"Have any men recovered on their own, or had milder cases?"

"Some are still alive after ten days, though I dare not name it recovered. Half, perhaps?"

"Hm. So, contagion, or contamination, do you think? Plague, or a poisoned well or the like?"

Rede's brows twitched up, as if the latter thought was new. By Adelis's jerk, it was an unwelcome idea to him, too. "I… Master Orides thought contagion."

I think Master Orides was correct, Des put in, thoughtfully. *Or at least on the right trail.*

Pen set aside the distracting memory of the famous possibly-poisoned well on the island of Limnos, which had historically destroyed an occupying army.

"Who were the first to fall ill? Is there any pattern?"

"Master Orides and I were puzzling over that. The first to die was our chief farrier, who'd been a strong man in excellent health. But the next was a quartermaster's clerk. Four foot soldiers. A cavalryman. A groom. Just last night, a laundress, the first woman. One of our own orderlies. And, now, our physician." That last seeming a heavier loss to Rede, and possibly to the fort, than all the rest combined.

"Any word of outbreaks in the village below?"

"The laundress was the first. I fear not the last. I've not yet had a chance to go down and ask."

"Someone should be sent for a census."

Adelis frowned, but nodded.

"So you…you are a sorcerer," said Rede, looking Pen up and down in perhaps justifiable doubt. "What can you do?"

So much. So little. Pen muffled a distressed sigh. "Have you ever worked with a sorcerer, or a Temple sorcerer-physician, before?"

"I'd never even met one. …Master Orides mentioned doing so once, but he didn't tell me much. Something about destroying the painful stones in the bladder."

"Ah. Yes. One of the easiest and safest procedures, and among the first taught. Much better than that thing with inserting the horrible spatula."

Rede nodded in a way suggesting he knew that ghastly technique first hand. Adelis, hah, cringed.

"The first thing you must understand is that my god-gift is *chaos* magic. It tends, and lends itself, most naturally to destructive procedures—downhill, it's dubbed. Of which there are more in medicine than one might think. But those can only clear the way for the body to heal itself, as the bladder cleans itself after the obstructing stones are rendered powder. Sometimes tumors can be destroyed." *Sometimes not.* "Intestinal worms also, though really, an apothecary's vermifuge does just as well." The wrenching urgent treatment for the fetuses misplaced outside the womb was the most delicate and advanced of all that downhill roster, and nothing Pen cared to discuss with the army physician. Or anyone else.

"So…is there then uphill magic?"

This boy is quick, Des purred in approval.

Pen nodded. "But it comes with a higher price than the downhill sort. A sorcerer can create order in, well, a number of ways, but then must shed a greater amount of disorder, somehow. If a sorcerer tries to do too much at once, or can't soon shed the excess of chaos, he or she is afflicted with a sort of heatstroke. Which can be as lethal as any other heatstroke."

"Oh. That, I had not heard of." Although from Rede's intent look, he understood and had undoubtedly treated heatstroke among the soldiers, no surprise in this climate. But then his nose scrunched up. "How in the world do you *shed chaos*? What does that even mean?"

Rede, Pen hoped, wasn't going to be a man baffled by technical vocabulary. He wouldn't have to water down his explanations.

"The area around the sorcerer suffers accelerated deterioration. Ropes fray or break. Metal rusts. Wood rots. Cups slip and spill or shatter. Sparks burn holes or set things alight. Wheels fall off, saddles slip, mounts go lame. The events aren't, usually, inherently unnatural, just their concentration and speed. Which is why an untrained hedge sorcerer is ill-advised to travel by ship, by the way." And then there were the tumors arising in the sorcerer's own body, which probably killed more inept sorcerers, in the long run, than uncanny heatstrokes. "Half my Temple training consisted of learning tricks to direct my demon's chaos safely outward to theologically allowable targets."

Rede was still listening intently, not interrupting this flow. Pen took a deep breath.

"The first magic my demon ever showed me was how to kill fleas and other insect pests. It turns out that the swiftest, most efficient sink of chaos is killing: the fall from life to death is the steepest slope of order to disorder that exists."

And the climb up it, as life built itself freely from matter in the world, its equally miraculous reverse. As Florina had just brought home to Pen most profoundly, but really, miracle was to be found in every breath and every bite of food he took, if he was mindful.

"So if I'm called upon to do much healing, I'll soon need to find some better sink for the chaos than a few bedbugs. We can deal with that later. The point is, my uphill magic doesn't cure or heal in a direct way. It fosters improved order in another's body so it may more speedily heal itself.

"So the other limiting factor, besides the need to find a chaos sink and the hazard of heatstroke, is how much help a body can accept at a time. I can no more force an injury to heal all at once than a man can eat a month of meals in a sitting. Repeated small applications are required.

"It follows that if the sickness is progressing faster than the body can digest my help, my attempt will fail. If the disease has gone past the point of no return, my magic will be wasted."

"You healed me," Adelis protested uncertainly. Rede glanced up at his commander's sober, scarred face, and his eyes widened in realization.

"I can heal a man. I can't heal an *army*. If many people end up afflicted, rationing my efforts is going to be required." Pen frowned unhappily at Rede. "We may be forced to choose my patients wisely and cruelly. As a legion's physician, you must know how that one works."

Rede rubbed his brow. By his matching unhappy frown, he was following this better than Adelis. "I've not yet attended on a battlefield, but Master Orides would sometimes speak of that problem, yes. If we could get him in his cups."

Pen nodded. "From the outside, my results look random, even though they're not. But when fears and hopes rule in such a hectic mash, it can generate unfortunate misunderstandings about my sorcery."

"You sound as if you speak from experience," said Rede. "Like Master Orides."

Pen gave a capitulating wave of his hand. "Two of my demon's prior riders were active physicians in the Mother's Order. Counting their whole careers both before and after they were gifted with a Temple demon, it adds up to something like ninety years of medical practice." Leaving aside his own fruitful, fraught five years of attempting the trade back in Martensbridge. "Given I'm only thirty-three, the effect can sometimes feel…odd."

Adelis's eyebrows rose at this. Had he never done the arithmetic?

An officer entered the far side of the courtyard, spotted Adelis, and headed determinedly toward him. Adelis shoved himself off the pillar to meet him partway; they conferred in low tones, then the fellow stood aside and waited. Adelis turned back to the pair on the bench.

"I need to attend to this. I'll leave you two to get on with it, for now, but report to me as soon as you have something substantive to add, Pen." For all the world as if Pen were one of his soldiers—score to Nikys.

Desdemona seized control of Pen's mouth. "Adelis, a word before you go."

"Hm? Is that you, Madame Desdemona?"

"Aye, boy."

Rede looked startled. "The demon speaks through his mouth?"

"Yes," sighed Pen.

Rede looked to his commander. "You can tell them apart? How?"

"Practice," said Adelis wryly. "I grant, some days I just give up and think of them as my sibling-in-law."

"Howsoever," said Des, for once unamused. "I'm going to let you conscript him for this, because halting him now would be hard. But you have to make me a promise in return."

"Oh?" said Adelis, with due caution.

"You've set him onto this road, so you have to tell him when to step off it. Because he won't be able to stop, and then we'll end up having another bloody argument about it. Shut up, Des." Pen closed his mouth with a snap. But she muscled in for a codicil: "You're the man in the saddle here, General Arisaydia, which even Pen must concede. This must be your load to lift."

"I am not much inclined to let a chaos demon dictate my duty, but I do take your point, Madame Des. We'll see."

"Evader," she muttered to his back as he trod off.

"But honest," said Pen. "One of his better traits, surely."

"Hah."

Rede had watched this exchange with increasing…not mistrust, exactly, nor disbelief, but maybe the wondering air of a man waiting for more evidence. True to his trade, that.

Pen clasped his hands between his knees, contemplating what must come next. First. Next-first. "Des, in your two centuries have any of you, physician or not, seen this particular sickness before?"

"Plagues and contagions, yes, but…" She shrugged with his shoulders. "There are only so many ways disease can break a body down. So the array of symptoms are for the most part familiar. That dire all-over bruising is the one new thing. Very diagnostic."

"The most urgent," Pen began, "no, the most important is to find out how it passes from its source to people, or from person to person if that's what it's doing. Right now, I need to test how much simple uphill magic can do. Which we'll only find out by trying it." He unfolded to his feet, Rede, after a tired moment, shoving up from the bench likewise. Pen added to him, "When we go back in, don't introduce me as a sorcerer. Just as a learned divine brought in by their general to pray for them. Which actually won't be a lie. But it would be very bad to raise false hopes at this stage." He added after a moment, "Or false fears. Some people have wild ideas about magic. And not just Quadrenes. I'm usually pleased to tutor anyone who will listen, but now isn't the time." And after another, "Except for you. You need to know."

"Yes," said Rede heavily, "I do. Show me."

Rede led him to the door of the next chamber past where his dead mentor lay. Pen thought to ask, "How many men brought into your care do you have still alive?" How far was he going to have to stretch himself?

"About thirty, at last report. Two more brought in this morning. Less one, now." His face set, doing this mortal summing.

Rede lifted the leather curtain, and Pen took a breath and forced himself across the threshold.

Six cots, again. One man was still able enough to be helped to the commode chair by two orderlies. Three of the afflicted were quite young soldiers, the others older but not old. Five times Pen knelt by cots and said, "Good day. I'm Learned Penric of the Vilnoc Temple, sent to pray for you," which was accepted without undue puzzlement, and once with a feeble smile and thanks. He made the tally sign over them, laid a palm on each flushed chest, murmured more rote blessings, and quietly let as much uphill magic as Des could produce wash into them.

The sixth man, skin purpling, his breathing labored, was bleeding from his nose and swollen eyes, being sponged clean by a worried orderly. He did not react to Pen's greeting. After a brief glance within his rotting lungs and gut by Sight, Pen just knelt and prayed.

Sweat was trickling down his back and beading at his hairline when Pen arose and motioned the closely watching Rede to follow him out. He headed straight for the fountain at the end of the court, where he washed his hands with the lump of sharp-scented camphor soap and, after a dubious glance at the much-used towel on its hook, shook them dry. He likewise passed over the common ladle hanging beside it, leaning in to guzzle straight from the bright stream, heedless of the splash on his garments. And then stuck his head under it, letting the flow cool his scalp. He was still panting when he straightened up again.

"And now," he wheezed to Rede, "I need to go find something to kill."

"I beg your pardon?"

"Stores. Grain stores would be good, or the stables. Or the midden. Anywhere rats or mice gather, or other vermin. Flies. Crows. Seagulls in a pinch, if any fly in this far from the harbor."

"Sometimes," said Rede. His stare was still doubtful.

"I don't need help for this part, if you need to get back to your tasks. Or some sleep."

"I…no. I want to see what you're doing."

To his patients as well, Pen guessed. "There won't be much to see."

Rede opened his hand. "Nonetheless."

"All right, then. Follow me."

Rede ended up leading, to the middens outside the most-downwind postern gate of the fort. The gate guard let the physician through without demur.

The manure pile lay to the left of the pathway, the kitchen waste to the right, both spilling down the slope of the fossa. The manure pile was much smaller than Pen would have expected for the number of horses, mules, and oxen kept within. He saw why in a moment—a villager at the bottom of the trench, shoveling up a load of good army rot into a hand barrow, to take off and spread on his garden or crops. Probably garden; if he'd wanted to manure a field he'd have brought a wagon. The flies were abundant on both piles, though no rats slinked about on this bright afternoon. He'd have to come back at night for those. Though a few crows and seagulls were picking over the kitchen trash, good.

Pen waited for the villager to turn away and start dragging his cart up the well-worn path on the far side of the big trench, then waved a hand. The faint buzzing over the pile died away. The flies dropped like, well, flies.

Rede stepped forward and stared down at the sprinkling of tiny, shiny black corpses. "That's disturbing."

"It took some getting used to for me as well, but I've had to feed my demon for fourteen years, now. It feels almost housewifely." *Feed* was a misnomer, the directed shedding of chaos being more a sort of elimination, but Pen had discovered that term went over much better with listeners than more messy material metaphors, all just as inaccurate.

That had been a lot of flies, but their tiny lives were not going to be enough for this. Also, Pen was now fresh out of flies. Glumly, he selected and dropped a crow as well, which fell over in silence. And without pain, there was that consolation. A couple of its curious comrades hopped over and stared down at it, understandably perplexed. Did crows grieve? Their god did, Pen knew. He tapped his lips with the back of his thumb in apology, to what or Whom he was not sure.

"That will do for the moment." Pen wiped his wrist over his cooling forehead. "But show me where the grain and food stores are, while we're over here."

Reentering, they were delayed by the gate guard demanding news of his sick squad mates. Rede, to his credit, gave a clear and honest, if brief, summation, though Pen wondered what distortions it would acquire when it came back off the soldier's tongue in barracks gossip tonight.

"I hope those idiots will bring themselves to me at once if they begin feeling ill," said Rede, looking back over his shoulder as they continued on to the grain stores. "The half who aren't malingerers to start with tend to claim they're just fine, no problems, sir, till they fall over. Master Orides says"—a hitch of breath—"said they annoyed him far more than the first sort."

Pen made five more trips between the hospice and the middens and stores before the late summer sunset. He examined, treated, and prayed over every sick man once, but by the time he visited the first chamber for the second time, the courtyard was dark and he was reeling and famished. Without demur, he let Rede guide him to the hospice staff's mess, where he wolfed down plain but abundant army food, and to a spare cot in the chamber where the orderlies slept. He wondered if it had belonged to the one who'd died.

"Is this helping them?" Rede asked bluntly as Pen flopped down on the wool-stuffed mattress.

"It's too soon to tell. Though sometimes you can only tell if it's too late. If a man dies, then it wasn't enough. If he recovers, would he have done so on his own?"

"Mm."

"I feel like a bucket brigade of one man, running back and forth from a well trying to put out a fire," Pen complained. "I need a bigger bucket. Or a closer well. A pump and hose. More men."

Could he get more men? There was only one sorcerer-physician he knew of in Orbas, serving the Mother's Order at Duke Jurgo's winter capital, but a more junior sorcerer might be conscripted for this, under Pen's supervision. The treatment was simple enough; not like the insanely finicky reconstruction of Adelis's acid-boiled eyes. Demons did not work well together, but they might be made to work in parallel.

I could manage to tolerate one, for this, Des told him. *How the other demon would fare, I can't guess.*

Gods, that was right, Pen needed to send a report on all this to his Order, and to the Mother's Order, in Vilnoc. It could be copied by scribes there and sent on to outlying chapterhouses. He should get up and go hunt quill and paper. He should.

"Has this thing broken out anywhere else, do you know?" he asked the shadowed ceiling. "Through army couriers or the like?"

"Not that I've heard. Master Orides was going to write to—oh, I should look through his papers. I don't know what he sent out before he was stricken himself."

Had Rede slept at all? Was he going to?

Pen compromised: "Have an orderly wake me at midnight. I'll make another round."

IN THE morning, after not enough sleep, Pen discovered that while the soldier who had been too far gone to treat had continued his journey to his god—though no others had died, yet—three more sickened men had been brought in. With such arithmetic, he wasn't getting ahead, here.

Also, one of Master Rede's orderlies had deserted in the night.

Rede swore in fury when he was told this over their hasty breakfast in the staff mess; not, it turned out, at the disloyalty or cowardice, but at the chance the fellow might have carried the contagion off to wherever he had fled to hide.

When he ran down from this muted tirade, he leaned his head back and asked either the plastered ceiling or Pen, "Which leads to the question, is this something a person gets only once, like some of the poxes, or is it something they could get over and over, like a catarrh or lung fever, with a chance of dying each time? Because if it's the first, I could safely press those who have recovered into service helping those who have fallen ill. Otherwise…"

Pen could only shake his head in equal doubt. Des, for once, had nothing to add.

Pushing himself up from the table, Pen began, again, the wearying round of prayer and magic alternated with hunting around in odd corners of the fort for more allowable vermin to slaughter. The manure-bred flies would take a few days to renew themselves, but seagulls, it appeared, flapped in routinely from the nearby coast, which might prove a reliable daily delivery. A seagull was worth a bit more than a rat, each of which was worth several mice, each of which was worth a few hundred insects. But if this went on much longer, he was going to need something more. Larger.

In between he ate, drank, and wrote urgent but frustratedly inconclusive notes to as many authorities as he could think of, for Adelis's military couriers to deliver. Adelis, when Pen handed these over to him in his headquarters map-room-and-scriptorium, had some disturbing return news carried by this same service. It had been sent from the fort and town at the far western end of the long east-west road spanning the duchy, which guarded the three-way border between Orbas, Grabyat, and Cedonia.

"From the description," Adelis said heavily, handing over the note for Pen to peruse, "it's the same Bastard-accursed thing we're having here. No disrespect intended to your god," he added as an afterthought.

Pen absently tapped the back of his thumb to his lips. "I think He accepts curses the way most gods accept prayers, really." He read the fort commander's terse description of their affliction, phrased less precisely than Pen would have put it but recognizable all the same.

Spurred, he sat down at the staff officers' writing table and composed a note to go with the next courier, to be given to the western fort's physician: briefly summarizing what had been happening here at Vilnoc, recommending they find a local Temple sorcerer if there was one, and giving his best guess so far of what such a mage might do to help.

"I wonder if this evil thing has turned up in Cedonia," Adelis remarked from his stool beside Pen, where he'd been watching this composition and giving unsolicited advice. He propped his elbows on knees and glowered at his sandals as if he could threaten them into an answer. "And how we could find out, or how soon."

For all that his natal country had so brutally exiled the general, Pen thought, pieces of his heart still anchored him there. Not, to be sure, with the Imperial bureaucracy, but rather with Lady Tanar and her household near the capital of Thasalon. Adelis's courtship of the young noblewoman had been disrupted by his arrest, blinding, and flight three years ago, but not, apparently, extinguished. A few secret letters had been smuggled across the border between them, Pen knew, because Adelis had shown them to his sister and mother.

"This isn't a hazard your sword arm could guard her from even if you were there," noted Pen.

"Is that supposed to be consoling?" said Adelis dryly.

"I suppose not. Though it's true."

"Hnh."

Pen's magic might help, but he had households much closer than Thasalon to concern him. "Have there been any reports of cases from the village besides the laundress?" Who had worked in the hospice. "Or from Vilnoc?"

"Not Vilnoc so far, five gods avert." Adelis made a less perfunctory than usual tally sign. "Some carters from the village, I'd heard."

Such men also frequently worked for the fort. Was there a connection? "I'd better go down and look at them, too."

Adelis frowned. "My men should come first."

Pen gave him a side-eye. "I serve my Order, and the archdivine. Not the army."

"They all owe allegiance to Duke Jurgo."

"The white god doesn't. Nor would the duke be wise to wish Him to."

Unable to gainsay this, Adelis just grunted.

A soldier came to the map-chamber door and called, "Sir, they're ready."

"Right." He rose and swung his red cloak over his shoulders; the soldier helped him set the bronze cloak-pin.

Pen followed them out, to discover that the reason for Adelis's military finery was the funeral just setting up at the temple across the main courtyard.

"Services for Master Orides," murmured Adelis. "Shall you attend?"

"I think my presence would distract your fort's divine, and Des would disturb the sacred animals."

Would not, protested Des. *But I suspect even Orides would prefer a more effective use of our time.* "We know he's gone to his goddess already," she added aloud.

Adelis glanced aside, as if trying to parse which one of them had spoken, then just shrugged.

Pen spotted Master Rede and a couple of his orderlies, who had also donned their military uniforms for this, trudging in from the direction of the hospice. Pen waved a hand at Adelis by way of farewell and angled toward them. Rede motioned his subordinates on, stopping by Pen.

"I'm about to walk down and take a look at any sick in the village," Pen told him.

"Oh. Good." Rede squinted in the bright sunlight. His eyes were bloodshot, but Pen trusted that was just fatigue and not a symptom. "Anything you can learn, bring back to me. I had a chance to look at Master Orides's papers. He'd been working on making a kind of list or grid of all who had come down with this thing, laying out everything known about them and looking for a pattern. I'm going to try to continue it later this afternoon."

"Sensible." Pen glanced across to the temple portico, where the sacred animals that signed which god or goddess had taken up the soul of the deceased were being brought out by their soldier-grooms. "You inter your dead whole here, yes?" A military cemetery lay outside the fort's walls, in the opposite direction from the village. "Should those who've died of this be cremated, instead, d'you think?"

Rede grimaced. "I just don't know. The weather is dry, so there should be no ground seepage from the cemetery. And wood is dear, if much would be required."

"In the cantons and the Weald, wood is abundant and cheap, but people still mostly bury." Des added as a cheery afterthought, "Except in certain special cases where burning is required to prevent spirit-possession of the corpse."

Rede looked taken aback. "That's real? Not a tale?"

"Death magic? Very rare, although dealing with it does fall as the duty of the Bastard's Order, so I was taught about it. Nothing I'd expect here."

"Glad to hear it."

Pen tapped his lips in either a blessing or a gesture of averting—with the white god, much the same thing—nodded wryly, and turned to make his way to the front gate.

IT WAS a short walk downslope to the dusty village of Tyno, which hugged, and hogged, the riverbank. It would have been shorter, but Adelis, when he'd taken over here two years back, had spearheaded one of the periodic removals of buildings that had encroached upon his defensive perimeter. This had not made him popular with the villagers, but since then his stern fairness, not to mention some compensation from Duke Jurgo's purse, had won the new general a grudging respect.

The main east-west road that—along with the river approaches to Vilnoc—the fort guarded ran through the upper outskirts of the village. Here clustered the taverns, Tyno's most lucrative trade; a few attendant inns, mostly for more modest visitors who couldn't afford lodging within Vilnoc's walls; and the brothels—prostitutes were among the Bastard's flock of human oddments, so in theory under Pen's care as a divine. A livery and a smithy also stood convenient to the road and its travelers.

Either would be tied into the town's gossip net. Smiths could run to either taciturn or usefully garrulous, but in either case were like to be busy. Liverymen, on the other hand, had to talk to their customers, and would also know where to find the sick carters. Pen strolled through the broad, open doors into the shaded stable. He left Des to snack on the available flies without his oversight.

A man advanced from the aisle between the straight stalls, propping a pitchfork aside and wiping his hands on his trousers. Ostler or owner, it didn't matter. "Good afternoon, sir," he began. "Whether it's a good riding horse or a nice, calm cart cob you're wanting, you've…five gods." He stopped short and stared wide-eyed at Pen, whose height, bright blond hair, blue eyes, and milk-pale skin were unusual for Orbas, if common in the cantons.

Or it's your pretty face, love, Des quipped.

Hush.

Thanks be for recognizable Temple vestments, or at least mercantile manners, because instead of falling into the usual wearying interrogation about Pen's looks, he recovered himself and went on, "Uh, learned sir? May I help you?"

"I hope so, although not to a horse, sorry. My name is Learned Penric, of the Bastard's Order in Vilnoc, and General Arisaydia asked me to examine the people who have fallen sick here lately of the strange bruising fever. A couple of carters, I was told, and perhaps others by now. Can you tell me names and where to find them?"

Arisaydia's status was even more useful here than the Order's, Pen guessed, because the man merely said, "Oh," and gave Pen directions to a house a street over.

"This bruising fever isn't one of our usual summer sicknesses," the liveryman added, swallowing uneasily. "Very fast and frightening, striking down grown men, not just the old or the infants. Does the Bastard's Order suspect a curse?" Holy or otherwise lay implied.

It wasn't an altogether unreasonable question, but it could be a dangerous rumor to let get started. "No," said Pen, more firmly than he felt. "It's a nasty disease, but there's nothing uncanny about it."

Agreed, said Des.

"But wouldn't a divine from the Mother's Order…"

"The fort's physicians are working hard," Pen diverted this. *True enough.* He decanted what the man knew of other sick folks here—three more households already, gods—and made his escape before he had to field further awkward speculations.

The carters' place, belonging to two brothers who lived together, lay in a row of houses that turned plain, whitewashed stucco faces to the street, not unlike a reduced village version of Pen's home. Pen knocked on the green-painted wooden door; waited; knocked again. He was just contemplating the horrid possibility that there was no one left alive inside, and if it would be acceptable to use Des's powers on the lock to intrude and check for corpses, when the door squeaked open.

An exhausted-looking middle-aged woman stared blankly up at him. “I…what?”

“Good afternoon, ma’am. I’m Learned Penric of the Vilnoc Temple. General Arisaydia asked me to look in on the ill folk here in the village.” All right, not quite what Adelis had said, but there was no harm in making him sound charitably concerned.

She looked Pen up and down. She evidently knew enough to read the details of his garb, for she said in some bewilderment, “Why did he send a sorcerer? If the Vilnoc Temple is trying to help, I want someone from the Mother.”

Des put in, before Pen could speak, “I’m married to his twin sister.”

“Oh,” she said, her inflection somehow combining surprise and reassurance. She opened the door to admit him.

What’s Nikys got to do with it? he asked Des, a little bewildered himself.

It worked. She’ll trust you across her threshold. Don’t complain.

Wouldn’t dream of it.

Fibber. You complain all the time.

Turnabout, fair play...

The carter's wife led him into the usual inner courtyard, ringed by the rooms of the house and used for every task from dining to sewing to washing, leatherwork, or minor carpentry. Right now, it was converted to a chamber for the sick, judging from the two beds of fine straw laid out on the flagstones. Upon them lay two men of sturdy build, but weak and flushed, glazed of eye. One redder than the other but not darkened to bruising yet; maybe Pen could still help? A basin of water and washrags, and another for vomit, sat between them.

"Is it only you to care for them?" Pen asked.

"My sister-in-law took all of our children to her mother's when we realized this was that thing from the fort."

"That...seems prudent." Or else it would spread the sickness to yet another household, but the deed was done and there was no benefit to worrying this woman further. It appeared the villagers had not, yet, taken to exiling the sick or their families beyond natural seclusion in their own houses.

Aye, plagues can get ugly far beyond their medical courses, Des remarked. From experience, Pen feared.

Contagion. Let's just call it a contagion, in front of people.

May be wise, for now.

While the woman knelt between the pair and took it in turns to bathe their faces with a wrung-out cloth, Pen sat cross-legged and asked all three about their recent activities.

The carters' latest venture out of Tyno had been to take an oxcart piled with the possessions of a retiring fort officer back to his home village, up a valley lying next-south from Vilnoc's. The trek had taken a week, but that had been nearly a month ago. Since then, they'd been busy locally, hiring themselves, their cart and their beasts to construction up at the fort.

"Could we have brought this thing back with us as hidden cargo?" asked the younger brother, the less feverish of the pair, uneasily. His elder winced.

"Given how recently you've been stricken, I don't think it," Pen reassured them. Truthfully, he hoped. "You should have been the first if that were so. No one else in your household has come down with it yet, right?"

They both looked at the woman, wife of the elder, in worry. She shook her head. This nurse would not desert her post, but it didn't mean she wasn't frightened. She added, "I wondered about the sheets. Because of the laundress." She gestured somewhat helplessly at the straw bedding. "This, we can burn later, but it's not what I like."

"Boiling the soiled sheets should suffice," said Pen. For the sheets and their next users, anyway. For the washerwoman handling them, it was less clear. "But there's nothing wrong with this straw arrangement, in this warm weather." Clever, actually; he'd have to suggest it to Rede.

The set of her shoulders eased at this endorsement.

Really, I am no authority to her, thought Pen, discomfited.

Do not waste our advantages on pointless humility, chided Des. *We may need every one before this is over.*

Mm.

Duly reproved, Pen merely smiled, and moved on to kneeling at each straw-bedside. There, in a spirit of theological redundancy worthy of a bridge-builder, he performed a prayer to all five gods, while covertly inserting as much uphill magic as they would take into each body. *Performing* seemed all too apt a term, but the audience, all three, seemed pleased enough with his delivery.

He wished he knew whether it was enough. He'd better not promise to come back, given the uncertainties up at the fort, but he wanted to try.

I know you do, said Des uneasily, *but this had better not become another hillside for you to die on.*

I am advised, he returned vaguely.

The sense of a snort.

"This is so strange," said the younger carter, frowning at the flush on his forearm discernible even through his sunbaked skin. "Do you think it was brought by those accursed Rusylli?"

Scowls all around at this conjecture.

"Have you heard of any sickness in their encampment?" asked Pen, alert. No one at the fort hospice had mentioned any, but then, their plates were full. Another place to check while he was down here? Adelis's name would not provide a glad welcome there, though his authority would get Pen in.

"No, but I haven't been out to the market for a few days," said the carter's wife. "My sister and neighbors have been leaving food at our door."

The older carter, peevish in his fever, growled, "I've told the youngsters not to go over there, but I know they do, when our backs are turned."

Pen's lips twisted in doubt. "But the Rusylli have been here, what, a year? If this was something they brought, it should have shown up much sooner." He drove home the point with, "Just as if it was something from your cart trip, it should have shown up later."

This was taken in with brooding looks, but no one tried to argue.

The batch of Rusylli prisoners of war from last year's campaign lived in an odd limbo, here at Tyno. Too important to sell off as slaves; not high enough to be held close as key hostages by Duke Jurgo's ally-in-law the High Oban of Grabyat. How Adelis had allowed himself to be lumbered with them, Pen was not sure. Nevertheless, several hundred Rusylli—minor tribal leaders and their immediate families—had been dropped downriver of Tyno and anchored there in a makeshift village by the expedient of the military engineers removing the wheels from their big house-carts.

Some people, Pen knew, romanticized the nomadic warriors. But then, some people romanticized *pirates.* Pen was not one of them, pirates on horseback seeming no more appetizing to him than the seafaring sort. As long as the Rusylli clans contented themselves with raiding each other, Pen had nothing to say to it, but when they took to preying on their settled neighbors, in western Grabyat and southwestern Cedonia, trouble started. Which kept men like Adelis employed, he supposed.

Des, in her prior lives in Cedonia, had not much encountered them. So even if not suffering from this malady, they might know something more, or at least other, than her long experience provided. Putative enemies, yes, but disease recognized no borders or boundaries. Rather like gods, that.

Pen hauled himself up and took his leave with a few more harmless sops of blessings all around, for which everyone seemed more grateful than Pen thought justified. He did not allow himself to frown in new thought until he had been seen out by the anxious wife and turned down the street, heading to the next stricken household on his list.

THE SUN was low by the time Pen emerged from the last of these, and he was overheated, fretful, and fatigued. The other families had offered the same maddeningly random assortment of victims, including one child. Pen had poured all he could into the boy, fearing it too little. He must squeeze time for a repeat visit to that household tomorrow, if no others. He hoped Rede would be able to make more of his observations than he did, so far.

He paused at the corner, needing to make a decision, which seemed slower in coming than it should.

That's because you need to decide to go eat, *Pen.*

Likely so. What he *wanted* was to go talk to the folk in the Rusylli encampment. But should he grab some bite from one of the nearby taverns, exposing them to whatever contaminations he might now bear, even if he ate it out of hand while walking down the river road? He wasn't sure if visiting the Rusylli after dark was a good idea. They'd be wary enough of him in daylight. Tomorrow morning might work better.

Return to the hospice mess, then, where they could all be contaminated together. He also very much wanted Rede to show him Orides's notes. He headed uphill in a weary trudge too like how his magic was starting to feel.

To Des's maternal approval, he got himself around some solid and abundant army food—*all the olives you can eat* wasn't that many for Pen, and he still could not like the dried fish planks, but the ox jerky and barley cakes were good, and the harsh red wine, once watered, more than acceptable. Sustained again, he tracked Rede down to Orides's writing cabinet adjoining the treatment rooms. Now Rede's writing cabinet, as the new commander of this careening disaster, though Pen wasn't quite sure if the man had assimilated that yet. Perhaps the funeral would have helped center him.

At Rede's beckoning, Pen sat down in the yellow lamplight of Orides's desk to share perusal of the late master's half-written reports on the autopsies and other case logs.

"Is an autopsy something you'd wish to repeat for yourself?" asked Rede, as Pen squinted at the inky scratches. He'd worked with worse handwriting on ancient manuscripts, but really, what was it about physicians? "Because we have a fresh body. The catapult sergeant died about two hours ago."

"Oh. I thought he might." Pen made the tally sign. "His internal disintegration did seem too far advanced to make anything of my help." Though Pen had tried, Bastard help him, in his last cycle through that sick-chamber. Just in case…

"But with Des's Sight, I don't need to open or even touch a body anymore to find out what's going on inside. Although my anatomical training, and Helvia's and Amberein's, were invaluable for putting a foundation to my understanding. Spirit-sight is not a match for what you'd see with your eyes or a magnifying lens, and it takes some practice to reliably connect the meaning of all those moving colors with their material substrate."

Rede sat back and stared at him with frank envy. "It sounds a wonderful skill for a Temple physician to possess."

No denying that; Pen shrugged. "Also, curiously, Des can tell contagion from poisoning, even when the gross symptoms are similar. Each can be diffuse, but there is something *alive* about contagion that poisons don't share. I keep thinking about that. Too diffuse for Des to separate, or it might be possible to kill the disease but not the person, the way I can kill fleas on a cat but not the cat. I like cats," he added muzzily. Gods, he was getting tired. Soon he'd be making no sense at all. This day felt a year long, and he still wanted to make another pass through the infected chambers.

Rede, charitably, ignored this last haphazard remark, unless he was growing as tired as Pen. But his black brows drew together in new thought.

"Could such a thing have to do with how the saints of the Mother effect their miraculous cures?"

Pen's heart lifted at this rare sign of understanding. "I've had that exact notion. A task too fine-grained for a man or even a chaos demon should not be too fine for a goddess. If ever I run across a saint of the Mother again, I want to ask"—if Des could refrain from going into conniptions at the divine proximity—"though it's possible the saint may not know. It's emptiness, not knowledge, that allows a person to channel a god. Howsoever, the Mother's Order in Vilnoc does not possess such a blessing, that I've heard." Although might the letters he'd sent off earlier today turn something up? It was too distracting a hope. "For now, we're on our own."

Rede nodded reluctant agreement.

Pen tapped the papers scattered across the table. "You've been observing this for longer than I have. Any thoughts? Speculations? Wild guesses?"

Rede scrubbed a hand through his scalp, spiky black hair overdue for a military haircut. "I don't think this disease starts in the lungs or the gut—those symptoms come last. It doesn't seem to travel in the breath, or people would have it in batches, especially in the barracks. Instead, it's one man out of dozens. Given all the vile things sick men emit, you'd think it would move in soiled linen, or vomit, or feces, but we've all been handling those, and only a few have taken ill. One laundress dead in three days, the rest fine, though several have refused to come back to work. I need to ask General Arisaydia to find us volunteers to help scrub. If there are not enough, conscript some, though that won't go happily."

"Mm."

"I've been thinking about the blood," Rede went on. "Master Orides would have been more exposed to that than anyone, during the autopsies."

"Did you assist at those?"

"I'd been detailed to other duties."

"Did anyone else, and have they been among the ill?"

Rede shook his head. "Once they'd set things up, Orides ran his helpers out. He said no one else needed to get that close."

Pen grimaced. "If you're asking if this disease is *in* the blood, yes, to be sure—the gross symptoms tell us that. Whether it starts there… I'll try to attend more closely to that question as I make my way around. Blood is peculiar stuff. Do you know it's still alive when it leaves the body, till it dries?"

Rede's brows flicked up in interest. "Oh?"

"I learned a lot about it, even beyond what most Temple physicians know, back when I took a year to train with the royal shamans of the Weald. Who use blood and the sacrifice of blood routinely in their magics, as demons use chaos and order. We had debates about connections, generally in their dining hall over late-night beer, but I can't say we found conclusions.

"I'm not sure where in my body my chaos demon is domiciled, but the shamans' Great Beasts definitely live in their blood. This has been known for a long time, which is why the execution of a shaman back in the days of the forest tribes used to involve hanging him upside-down and butchering him like a hog. They believed it drained him of his powers with his blood."

"That...would work on anybody, really," Rede pointed out.

A spurt of laughter escaped Pen's lips. "True. Anyway. This bruising disease does seem alive in the blood, not unlike those lethal infections that sometimes follow wounds. ...Though the shamans would be quite offended to have their Great Beasts dubbed a blood disease."

"I'll keep that in mind, should I ever meet one." Rede had a dry humor hidden in there, if battered at the moment.

They turned once more to Orides's writings, coming to the end too soon, like their author. The case notes, meticulous in the beginning, grew ever more abbreviated. *Bastard's teeth, another one*, read one of the last. The physician's observations seemed keen to Pen, but included nothing he hadn't seen for himself by now.

Pen bit his lip and sat back. "Were you able to make anything of that comparison-grid he'd started?"

"I added the newer cases to it. They're all over the map, or at least all over the fort. I ranked the numbers by company. There may be a slight bias to the cavalry, but that doesn't explain the laundress. Or the people in town. Oh. I should include them." He scratched in Pen's accounting from the village and handed the page across to Pen.

Indeed, any clustering seemed slight. "I suppose more numbers might make it clearer, but that's not something to wish for."

"Five gods avert," said Rede. And then, after a pensive moment, "Do They?"

"Not that I can tell," sighed Pen. "I've sometimes wondered if the gods regard death not as a dreaded ending, but as a welcome beginning."

"Of what?"

"I am deeply not sure. Which doesn't stop people from making up a thousand tales." Or maybe the gods provided a thousand versions, tailored to each soul. Pen wouldn't put it past Them. "There doesn't seem to be any need to rush to find out, though. The gods wait all the same."

Rede signed himself; Pen didn't bother. They both shoved up to return to the sick-chambers.

PEN WASHED himself the next morning at the hospice courtyard fountain, stripping to the skin and applying the camphor soap liberally, including his hair. His summer vestments, much the worse for the past two days, he tossed into a bucket for Des to deal with. The price of even a few insect lives for his laundry seemed dimly wrong to Pen, but this was a special case.

Even with Des's help, he didn't think he could wash *enough* to risk returning to his Vilnoc home, and Nikys and Florie and Idrene, not until they'd come to understand how the bruising disease passed from person to person. When he'd answered Adelis's plea for aid, Pen had not anticipated so profound an exile.

He shook out the de-bloodstained whites for Des to speedily steam dry, trusting the passing orderlies would be too distracted by their duties to notice his odd activities, redonned them, and fastened his hair back in a simple queue. Slipping on his sandals, he clipped off to find Adelis.

He tracked the general down in his quartermaster's office. At Pen's wave, Adelis interrupted his business and came to the doorway. Pen led him out under the colonnade.

"Have you heard of any cases of the bruising fever in the Rusylli camp?" Pen began. "Master Rede hadn't."

"Hm. The quartermaster's grain deliveries to them are made weekly, and one of their tasks is to report back to me on the state of affairs there. So not unless something has popped up in the past few days, no."

"I'm going to walk down there and see if they know anything about this disease that we don't."

Adelis shrugged. "I shouldn't think they'd be very willing to talk to you, but I suppose you can try. Hold a moment, and I'll detail you some guards."

"I don't need them, surely. I mean…*we* don't."

"I don't underestimate your ability to defend yourself, Penric. Yourselves. But the presence of a few of my men will reduce the temptation to ambush you, avoiding the problem in the first place."

"Mm, and doubtless make the Rusylli even more closemouthed. I think not."

Adelis plainly misliked this plan. "Then take my translator. The Rusylli have several of their own Cedonian speakers, but at least you'll be able to know if what you're told is what is actually being said."

"Same problem, and also not needed. All those Cedonian language lessons I gave to Rybi the Rusylli girl last winter didn't just go one way."

"Really?" Adelis's brows rose. "I thought you inherited your gifts of languages from Madame Des."

"I did, but I haven't let them lie fallow and uncultivated. Also, it turns out languages are like children. Once you have six, adding a seventh hardly makes any difference. Or so my mother used to say." He added after a moment, "Me being her seventh, you know."

"I'll take her word for it." Adelis's mouth ticked up at the corner. "Report back to me if you learn anything new."

"Of course." Pen escaped before Adelis could come up with more objections. To be fair, the man wasn't just being a fusspot. He'd been ambushed by Rusylli a *lot.*

Pen made his way out to the main road and turned right, thinking about Rybi. Adelis had dumped the pregnant Rusylli girl upon Pen's household—well, upon Idrene, whom he knew would be sympathetic to her plight—late last fall. She'd had a drearily familiar story: a soldier-lover from the fort, forbidden trysts, predictable consequences. Accusation on her side, denial on his, and a family who had beaten and forcibly ejected her. The uproar had worked its way up to Adelis, who didn't have any more luck sorting out the truth than anyone else. Pen thought he and Des might have, given some time with the boy, but the Father of Winter, not the Bastard, was the god of justice, and Adelis's army was not any responsibility of Pen's. Although somebody had to be detailed to clean the latrines, and Adelis, for so many reasons not appreciating the ruckus one bit, had made sure the soldier's officers knew who.

The anguished girl had slowly recovered over the ensuing months, bruises both physical and mental fading under Idrene's and Nikys's care. The Rusylli had no writing, so Pen had weighed in with lessons in both the Cedonian language, and reading and letters, in return for all those household chores. She'd given birth to a healthy boy about a month before Nikys had delivered Florina. Nikys had no need at all for a wet nurse, so Pen had found Rybi a place doing that at the Bastard's orphanage in Vilnoc, where she and her child were well-fed, safe, and very welcome. She still returned to Pen's house once a week for language lessons—not just hers, but his.

Rybi had taught him quite a bit about the nomads' lives and customs, along with their vocabulary and peculiar grammar. Sadly, nothing about it led Pen to believe that mentioning his care of her would be of aid in the encampment, and more likely the reverse.

I think you're right, said Des. *Also, if they offer you a translator, it might be wise to conceal your command of their tongue, as well as how you acquired it. For much the reasons Adelis said.*

Eavesdropping, Des? It was a ploy that had served Pen well a time or two before, true. *We'll see.*

After a ten-minute walk down the road, a somewhat denuded grove of trees hove into view. It sheltered a collection of huts, formerly wagons, fifty or sixty of them. On this clear morning, the shafts of light filtering through the branches and the bright sun-dapple spangling everything made the place look more idyllic than it likely was.

Pen turned in past the cursory guard post kept there, just four soldiers. At least one of them recognized not only his vestments but Pen as the general's sorcerous brother-in-law, because he braced and gave a military salute, saying nervously, "Learned sir. Sir." With Adelis's army brutes, Pen was never sure if this intimidation was from the brother-in-law or the sorcery part.

Pen returned a tally sign, and murmured, "Five gods' blessings upon you all. I'm on an errand for Adelis," and marched past, avoiding delays for interrogations, gossip, or anxious inquiries about what was happening in the hospice that he really couldn't answer.

A few people were about, tending to chores in the shade. An occasional goat, chicken or pig wandered among them. A dog scratched itself and lay back down with a tired whuff. The army had seized their hostage-prisoners' draft animals—oxen and beloved horses—for much the same reason as they'd removed the wheels from their traveling huts, but had left the smaller food animals. Pigs, ill-suited to keeping up with wide-ranging herds, were not normally a steppe meat, so Pen presumed they'd been added later. The Rusylli had no other objections to pork, being happy enough to steal it while raiding outlying farms, though horses and young women were more prized. At least they didn't eat the last.

Pen's arrival was noticed at once. Pen was inured to being stared at in the street, but not usually with such hostile suspicion. Though it wasn't for his coloration; particularly in the far south, the Rusylli clans had their share of blonds and redheads, possibly a legacy of all those stolen wives.

A half-dozen sturdy men assembled on the rutted entry road. Bows and swords had been taken from them, of course, but the army had perforce left them knives and butchering tools. And cudgels, Pen knew, could bash sorcerer skulls just as well as they did ordinary ones. The men weren't heavily armed; they just looked as if they wished they were. They wore a motley combination of traditional dress—well-fitted, bright-patterned weaves, leather straps, metal ornaments—and Orban army castoffs, variously mended.

Des commented, *I wonder if their reputation for screaming into battle dressed in nothing but riding chaps and tattoos is less bravado than their wives and mothers objecting to the wear, tear, and bloodstains on their shirts?*

Not in the steppe winters, they don't. Which Pen understood could get even more bitterly cold than his mountain cantons.

Around the encampment, a scattering of young women and girls whisked or were whisked into the huts. The old crones kept working, though they watched the proceedings narrow-eyed. A few young boys took up idle poses, and didn't even pretend not to stare in curiosity. Pen wondered if they included some who'd sneaked out to play with the carter children along the riverbank.

Pen really wanted to talk with the old women, but apparently these mature men were who he was going to get. They were all here in the first place, Pen was reminded, because they were leaders who were disinclined to make peace.

"Good morning," Pen began in Cedonian as they all stopped within speaking range. "Five gods bless and keep you." He offered a tally sign, which was taken in with neither delight nor offense. The vagaries of Rusylli theology were a whole other dissertation, but they did recognize Pen's god as one of the Five, not an abject reject of Four as the Quadrene heresy would have Him. Or Her, or Him-Her, depending on the tribal region; for a bodiless, if vast, being of pure spirit, Pen granted that the assignment of sex was arbitrary. These men could decode Pen's Orban vestments, anyway. "I need to talk to someone."

One of the group shouldered forward. Middle-aged—by Rusylli standards, which probably meant he was about as old as Pen—missing his right arm, so not a bowman or warrior. Anymore. He lifted his bearded chin at Pen.

"I'm Angody. I speak Cedonian."

"Thank you." Pen bent his head in a polite nod. He gestured to a circle of stumps and logs around a nearby cold firepit. "May we sit? This might take a bit." Once seated, Pen would be harder to eject.

Angody glanced to another man, taller and with brown hair and beard in ornamented braids, who nodded permission. So, the translator was follower or retainer, not leader. They all shuffled over and settled themselves, not comfortably, but that wasn't due to the makeshift furniture.

"Should I get a woman to fetch drinks?" another man, more warrior-like or at least still in possession of all his limbs, asked the leader in low-voiced Rusylli.

"No. Maybe he'll go away sooner."

A nod of understanding, and the fellow sat cross-legged and straight-backed, frowning at Pen. Guests were normally plied with food or drink in Rusylli camps; Pen, having heard vivid descriptions of these treats from Adelis, was just as glad to be spared the need to politely choke down, say, fermented mare's milk.

Which they don't have anyway, since their mares were taken away, Des pointed out. *We're safe.*

Hm.

"My name is Learned Penric. I serve the Bastard's Order in Vilnoc," Pen began. He paused, but no return introductions were forthcoming. As they seemed to be skipping opening pleasantries, he continued directly: "Master Rede, the physician at the fort, wanted me to ask around. A number of his men have been taken with a strange fever, unknown in Orbas. Or Cedonia, or anywhere in the countries easterly, for that matter."

He paused while Angody converted this to Rusylli, with tolerable accuracy. No reaction from the other men. Pen went on, "It begins as an ordinary fever, but then progresses to bleeding, under the skin, in the gut and lungs, and finally even from the nose, ears, and eyes. The skin all over darkens like a bruise—well, it is a bruise, technically—toward the end. It's very painful."

Angody's brows went up, and he repeated this, more rapidly. *Now* his listeners all flinched back.

"We've started dubbing it the bruising fever, for lack of any other information, but it must have a name *somewhere.* Wherever it comes from. Is this anything the Rusylli know, or that you've heard or even heard rumors about?"

"The blue witch," muttered one man. "Her curse has come *here?*"

The braid-bearded man motioned him to silence.

"What should I tell him?" Angody asked the leader.

"Tell him nothing. Tell him we know nothing. Those army curs are always willing to believe that."

"I don't think this one is that stupid," said Angody. "And not army. These eastern Temple-men are bookish fellows, aren't they?"

"That doesn't make them any less witless," put in another man, the eldest if the sprinkling of gray in his beard was anything to go by. "Just more nearsighted."

"Maybe we'll be lucky and they'll *all* be cursed," another said with venom. "The demon general first."

A moment of weirdly respectful fear slithered through the circle at this mention of Adelis. When Adelis had come back from his blinding as if risen from the dead, face exotically scarred and eyes turned garnet red, both enemies and allies found him newly alarming. Never a man to waste either time or an advantage, Adelis accepted this addition to his command mystique and let the fantastical rumors proliferate. His private feelings, no one witnessed save his sister and mother. And Pen, as his intimate healer.

"Yes, let our wicked foes be punished," agreed the ill-wisher's seatmate on his log, in piety of a sort Pen supposed.

"Now you're talking foolishness," said Graybeard. "The blue witch has neither friends nor mercy. She takes men as blindly as a madwoman picking flowers."

Braid-beard nodded grim agreement. "And if she's *there*, she could come *here*."

Pen kept his expression bland and mildly inquiring as he looked to Angody.

Angody blinked at his leader and said to Pen, "It sounds very frightening. But we don't know it."

"You've had no such sickness here in this camp?"

"No," said Angody firmly. Not lying about that, at least. A man could make the five-fold tally as well with the left hand as the right, and Angody did. Although if the gods could avert any of this, Pen had seen no sign of it.

Des's sly ploy had paid off, Pen had to grant her that. He wouldn't be getting the half of this if the Rusylli knew he understood what they were saying. And he had the main information he'd come for; that the bruising fever hadn't broken out here at all, let alone first.

Should he interrogate them further, revealing his eavesdropping? It sounded as though their understanding of the disease was shot through with wild tales, which however interesting to Pen as a scholar were of little use to him as a physician.

Perhaps not, said Des in doubt. *Though odd clues do turn up in strange dress sometimes, in diagnoses.*

Pen wanted more, but either coercing or tricking it from such reluctant informants would take him time and energy that thirty-five men in the hospice and a little boy in town could not spare. He contented himself with a, "Well, if you think of anything else, or hear of anything further, please send a message to me at the fort by way of one of the gate guards. They'll be able to find me. I'm very interested. And *especially* if anyone here comes down with it. That would be a matter of utmost urgency. I can help."

Which…was not yet proved. Upon Angody translating this, it didn't look as though they believed him anyway.

Pen rose and took his leave of the Rusylli men with another polite blessing. They walked him almost to the road, seeing him out. Or off.

He was, to no surprise, now accosted by the gate guards wanting news of their comrades in the hospice. Trying to strike a balance between reassurance and honesty was awkward, but at least Pen was able to put in an authoritative word or two absolving these Rusylli of having anything to do with it, which might help prevent future trouble.

Pen strode back toward Tyno wondering if that was really true.

"Hey. Hey. God man," he was hailed in a sharp whisper from the verge.

He wheeled and paused. The speaker crouching half-concealed in the weeds stood up. A Rusylli woman, by her dress and ornaments; older, a near-crone, work-gnarled but still hale, by the way she sidled up to him. She was guarded, or dogged, by a thin hound, its muzzle gray to match her head. It leaned into her skirts, watching Pen as anxiously as its mistress. Her hands flexed, as if wanting but afraid to grasp him.

"Rybi. Rybi. Demon general took. Alive? Dead? *Rybi*," she said in broken Cedonian.

Bastard be thanked. Making an instant decision, Pen returned in reasonably smooth Rusylli, "The girl Rybi? Who left your camp last fall? Who are you to ask after her?"

At hearing her language, a look of relief crossed the woman's worn features, and she came back with a term in Rusylli that meant something like a maternal sister of an older generation; *great aunt*, Pen decided, was close enough. He'd get the nuances from Rybi later. She went on, "They say the general took her away. They say she died."

"She's alive."

"Where? How?" If Pen's summer tunic had possessed a sleeve, he thought she would have tugged it in her urgency.

"Given that her brothers half-killed her, while her father egged them on and her mother did nothing, I'm not sure I should tell her family where to find her to finish the job."

Taking this in, she nodded grimly. "It goes that way, sometimes."

That particular flavor of sexually charged brutality was by no means unique to the Rusylli, although whether the neighbors condoned or condemned it varied from people to people. Pen was glad his god was implicitly on the side of *condemned.*

"I gather that she crawled off to die in front of the fort gates by way of reproach, which is how she came to General Arisaydia's attention." He'd near-tripped over her, by the tale he'd told Idrene and Nikys. "I can tell you she's recovered, doing well, and in a safe harbor." Should he mention the healthy infant, or would that just multiply the targets?

"Can you speak to her?"

Cautiously, Pen chose, "I might be able to relay a message."

"Then tell her, her Auntie Yena cares for her still. Tell her, live and be well. Don't come back. Don't look back." She nodded decisively.

Rybi had pretty much figured all that out for herself by now, Pen thought, except for the part about her aunt's regret, so he merely said, "I will."

A huff of relief.

Pen, murmured Des. *Don't waste this opportunity.*

God-given or no, right. "I didn't come out here about Rybi. I came to ask about a disease that has turned up in the fort, that I hear is known to the western Rusylli people. The men wouldn't speak to me of it. Will you?" She stood poised, tense, but not running off, so Pen again went on to describe the bruising fever. "They named it the blue witch, or the curse of the blue witch; it wasn't clear how they thought of it. Though I can say with confidence that there's nothing uncanny to it. It's just a disease, if a gruesome one."

Yena scowled, taken aback. "Is that so, god man? I've never seen it myself. I've met folk who lived through it."

So, people were known to survive it; encouraging. "Oh?"

"Sometimes it killed whole camps, they say, out in the far west. Sometimes only one or two folk. But only in the summer. Other sicknesses kill us in the winter. The survivors are shunned, so they stay with each other, as best they can."

Alone on the steppes was a good recipe for *dead on the steppes*, Pen had no doubt. "I see. Important question: do you know if people get it just once, or more than once?"

Her brow wrinkled. "I've never heard of anyone stricken with the blue curse twice. If they're weakened enough, they sometimes die of other things later." She shrugged. "As do we all. Though the warrior lads don't want to hear of it, as if death in battle is the only one that counts."

"The five gods count them all, Auntie Yena."

"Do they, now." Her first worries quelled, she stared him up and down with more open curiosity.

"I'm sure of it."

Her lips pursed. "The red-eyed general—do you know him?"

"Uh, yes?"

"Is it true he commands demons?"

Not exactly. There's only the one, though she'll do him favors now and then. If he asks nicely and she feels like it. Probably more detail than Yena needed. "No. He's not a sorcerer. Temple or hedge." Did she not realize that Pen was? He was becoming unsure, but it would explain her boldness.

"Huh." Her gaze flicked toward the grove, and back. Her voice dropped to a rough whisper. "Will he ever let us go?"

Adelis, Pen knew, would be delighted to be rid of the Rusylli clan—actually, portions of four different clans—dropped on his doorstep. It doubtless wouldn't do to say it so bluntly. Pen temporized, "It's not up to General Arisaydia. He obeys Duke Jurgo, who keeps you as a favor to his ally Grabyat. If your countrymen ever stop raiding across the Uteny River, maybe the High Oban will relent." *Not up to me, either*, Pen hoped she understood. If not, time and people being what they were, a century from now this encampment might be just a village of Orbas with a population that spoke an odd dialect.

She grunted at this unhelpful, if true, answer, then looked over her shoulder, as though afraid of being spied out from the grove. Granting Pen a short nod—half salute, half thanks—she scurried away into the scrubby trees, her skinny old dog at her heels.

Pen walked on, his mind churning.

THE LITTLE boy in the village was still alive this morning, Pen discovered to his relief when he diverted to stop in and check him. If uncomfortable, whiny, and restless, possibly a good sign; he'd been panting and quiet yesterday. Another prayer-treatment seemed to be smoothly absorbed. Because she was right there, he went on to minister to his feverish servant mother, and then, unable to forbear, made the rounds of the three houses he'd visited yesterday. If only to examine and record what changes his simple magics had produced so far, he persuaded himself.

No one had died in the night; no one was obviously on the road to recovery. In the course of this, he learned about a fourth household stricken, a family of tanners, so he visited them, too. By the time he made his way wearily back up the hill to the fort, body too hot and demon too tense, it was past noon, much later than he'd intended to be. Arriving at the hospice, he discovered that Rede's thirty-five patients had grown to forty.

I can't do *this*, was his first dismayed thought.

Or, came his second, not with what scant vermin remained in the fort from his prior hunts. It was time to arrange a more reliable chaos sink. Which was going to be awkward at best and at worst did not bear thinking about. He trudged off to find Adelis, who, for a change, was actually in his headquarters.

"How did it go with the Rusylli?" Adelis asked at once. "I see you still have your ears." One of the less grisly trophies Rusylli warriors took from their enemies; more portable than heads, Pen supposed.

"Oh, yes," sighed Pen. "As you guessed, they were not forthcoming, but I was lucky." He detailed his visit, and its unexpected codicil with Rybi's aunt. Adelis planted his elbows on his writing table, folded his fists, and rested his mouth against them, stemming interruption till Pen was finished.

"The upshot," Pen concluded, "is that the bruising fever may have come from the Rusylli tribes, or at least from the far western steppes, but not from your Rusylli. It is named, but not explained. By the way, I suggest we call it something other than *the blue witch.* That's the sort of thing that could get perfectly innocent black-haired hedge mages murdered by their neighbors."

"I see." Adelis frowned.

"There were two more cases in the village last night," Pen went on, "and five more of your men reported in to Master Rede. If I'm to go on, Des must have a better way to shed our discharge. Your fort cooks kill far more animals in a day than I ever could. I need you to order them to let me do some of their slaughtering."

Adelis's forehead wrinkled like some wine-inked topographical map. "As you do for my sister in her kitchen?"

A few times a week, depending on the menu, Pen relieved the scullion of the chore of killing the chickens, ducks, pigeons, or rabbits bought live in the market and destined for roasts or stews, depending on the age, price, and stringiness of the meats. Adelis had on occasion watched with fascination. He'd had the theological lecture often enough that he'd stopped asking Pen, somewhat enviously, why he couldn't do this to enemy soldiers. "Yes, but scaled up."

"I must say, I was impressed by that thing Des does with the feathers. One pop, and you have a bag of feathers and a naked bird to hand to the cook. Very efficient."

"I am not using my demon to pluck chickens for your army, Adelis." *Thank you*, murmured Des. "Time is of the essence here, or at least, my time is. The point is, people who are unaccustomed to me and my magics can get very disturbed by my processes. I had a special arrangement with a Martensbridge butcher, back when I was practicing medicine regularly there, and even he kept my visits, well, not quite secret, but private from his customers. A kitchen that serves several thousand meals a day being what it is, there's going to be nothing private about this."

"Yes, the place is a maelstrom." Adelis's eyes narrowed. "Hm. I think I have a solution for that. Let's go."

Pen found himself trotting after the general's quick tread, threading through the fort to the side that housed the soldiers' mess and the kitchen courtyard. The latter was much less serene than the hospice courtyard, crowded with its own fountain, an array of brick ovens, several firepits for slow-roasting large carcasses that were smoking aromatically, and a lot of scurrying men, shouting and swearing.

A pool of startled attention formed ahead of Adelis, closing to uproar again as he passed through, like water around the hull of a ship. He tacked off to the colonnade, under which they found an open chamber filled with writing tables, invoices, accounts, and a harried mess-master and clerks.

"Sir!" The mess-master rose and saluted Adelis. He was a swarthy, scarred, and grizzled fellow who'd come up through the ranks of army cooks, Pen guessed.

"Good afternoon, Sergeant Burae. This is my brother-in-law, the Temple sorcerer Learned Penric. I've assigned him the task of slaughtering the chickens and whatnot for the officer's mess tonight. I've watched him do this at his home. The animals that die serenely and calmly in the arms of his god taste much superior to those which die struggling in pain and terror."

No, they don't, said Des. *They're all the same.* Though Pen was just as glad that his food didn't have to suffer further for its sacrifice to his table.

"Mind, these are to be reserved for officers only," Adelis emphasized. "Don't get them mixed up with the men's mess."

Burae looked confused but impressed. Pen muted a grin, and Des said, *Ah.* Clever *lad. By tomorrow, they'll be begging you to kill their poultry, and sneaking it away for the kitchen rowdies to sample.*

"I'll leave you two to get on with it," Adelis finished. "Penric will tell you what he needs."

"Sir!" The mess sergeant saluted again as Adelis took his leave. He turned more uncertainly to Penric. "Learned sir…?"

Burae led Pen through an arch in the colonnade to the kitchen's slaughtering space, a tiny courtyard open to the sky, paved with flat stones angled toward drainage channels. A pair of kitchen lads were engaged in dispatching crates of doomed poultry through the traditional method of grabbing the bird by the head and swinging it vigorously around, snapping its neck in the instant, until the body flew apart from it, wings still flapping wildly for a minute or so. Even for young rowdies like these boys, the novelty of this entertainment had clearly faded after the first few thousand chickens.

"This fellow is the general's tame sorcerer," Burae told his lads, evidently all the introduction he thought they needed. "He's here to kill the chickens for the officers' mess. Somehow." His stare at Pen was very doubtful.

To make it apparent to his agog observers that he was actually doing something, Pen made the tally sign, tapped his lips, and waved his hand beneficently over the remaining birds. Three dozen chickens fell over silently in their crates.

Ohh, said Des, a very corporeal-seeming sigh. *Oh, that helps* so much. Pen controlled a perfectly imaginary urge to belch.

More? Pen inquired.

Bastard avert, no. How would you feel if you ate that many chickens at a sitting?

That seemed all they could do on one visit, then. *How long do you think it will last us?*

A hesitation. *Maybe not forty men.*

Or however many had turned up at the hospice by now. *Understood.*

"That's all I can do at present," Pen told Burae. "I'll be back later this afternoon. Please save me some work if you can. About that much again."

Bewildered but, thanks to Adelis and habits of army discipline, pliant, Burae nodded and saw his visitor out. Pen winced to imagine the garbled kitchen and barracks gossip that was going to arise from this episode.

He headed back to the hospice court. Really, if this worked out smoothly enough, he might not have to visit the fort's main abattoir, located outside the walls. There the large animals, cattle and pigs, were slaughtered; hides, horns and hooves removed and sent to the tannery and other local workshops, dismembered joints carted up to the fort ready for the cooks to further break down into the dozens of ways every bit of an animal was used. Skipping the slaughterhouse would be fine by Pen. He was keenly aware that he was good at this task, but he disliked it and was happy to leave such killing to other men. Rather like the practice of medicine, with which, for him, it was so weirdly, intimately bound. Not a useful thought right now, that.

REDE'S FORTY patients had grown to forty-one by the time Pen, still not done working through the initial roster, had to break off due to overheating and Des's growing frenzy. Back at the fort kitchen, he discovered that its mess-master had found time to collect gossip and think.

"You've been working in the hospice." Standing up to Pen, Burae sounded scared but stern. "I don't want sick men in my good kitchen. No matter what the general thinks about his dinner."

"I'm not sick, but I appreciate your point," said Pen, startling Burae a trifle; had he imagined Pen would argue? But Pen needed his food animals, or some animals. "I can think of two compromises. You could have your lads bring the crates of creatures to the courtyard entry, and I wouldn't have to come within. Or, better"—from Pen's viewpoint, as he didn't want to be putting on a show for every passerby—"if there's a back entry to the slaughtering room, I can use it."

"There is," said Burae slowly. "I suppose at least you wouldn't be trailing through our whole working space."

"Good thinking."

Partially reconciled, the mess-master led out and roundabout to show Pen the delivery door. The lads had reserved him a couple of crates of rabbits, which would do nicely, rabbits being, for some reason, an even better sink than poultry. Someday, when he had time to think, Pen wanted to work out a creature-ranking for this effect to see if it would reveal an underlying pattern, but today was not that day. By its end, he'd probably be too tired to walk, let alone think.

Des's burden relieved, Pen headed back to the hospice, wondering about scheduling. Slaughtering was normally a morning task for the kitchen, and it looked as though he'd be working the night around.

They start very early, said Des. *Still night by your scholarly standards. And even you must sleep sometime.*

I suppose…

THE FORT'S officers having not fallen over poisoned in the night due to sorcerous meddling with their food, Burae seemed less worried the next morning, leaving his lads with Pen to carry on. As a result Pen spent a long, miserable, unimpeded day ferrying death back and forth across the fort. He was able to slip down to the village once, in the late afternoon.

One sick woman, an acolyte at the village temple and so better educated than most, twigged to the fact that Pen was delivering magic along with his prayers. Either Pen's forced explanation reassured her, or fear of the fever proved greater than her fear of sorcery. But the news, necessarily decanted in front of the sister who was caring for her, would be all over the village by tomorrow. Would the infected households turn him away in alarm? Pen wasn't sure what he'd do then.

Let 'em rot, advised Des, her crankiness hinting she was getting to her limit again. *You've no shortage of other work.*

You know we can't stop. If anyone I've touched or even come near dies, they won't blame the disease for killing them, but me for not saving them. Or worse, as rumor chewed and spat out frightened nonsense.

Don't borrow trouble. The interest rate is much too high. One day at a time, here, Pen.

Or one hour. He shook his head and trudged uphill again.

UPON RETURNING to the hospice court, Pen traced Rede to one of his treatment rooms, wondering what fresh bad news the physician might have to impart. He found Rede with a small pile of bandage scraps, scissors, and a flask of wine spirits, suggesting he'd just concluded some wound care, but standing scowling down into a high-sided wooden box on the table. Approaching to look over his shoulder at the source of his displeasure, Pen discovered it contained a large, elderly, and very sick rat.

The mangy creature lay on its side, panting in irritation, not even trying to escape. Some rats, if they were young and healthy, could be rather attractive little animals, bright-eyed and inquisitive. This…was not a cute rat.

"Is that for me?" asked Pen, a trifle confused. "Because I'm not looking for more rats, now that I've worked out my arrangement with the kitchen. But I can kill it for you if you like."

"No!" said Rede, with a sharp deterring gesture. "Don't. I want to save it."

"Er…did you want Des to heal it, then?"

Rede cast him an exasperated look. "Of course not. I want to save it to watch. Study."

"Where did you come by it? I didn't think I'd left a rat or a mouse alive in the whole fort."

"A soldier brought it in. Quartermaster's clerk. He'd been bitten. In the archives, where he'd gone to hunt up some record or another. Rats and mice lurk there—going after the old parchment, probably. He saw the beast was sick, so he caught it in a cloth and brought it to me along with his bleeding arm. In case I could tell anything. He was worried it might have given him some disease, maybe the bruising fever. I can't see if the wretched thing is bruised or not, though." He glanced aside at Pen. "Can you?"

"Uh..." The creature had dark fur, what there was left of it, and black skin, except for its pale feet. In the bruising fever, the extremities darkened first. *Des?*

Really, Pen. The things you ask of me. A pause. *Fevered, yes. Bruised, no. Apart from where it was manhandled in its capture.*

"Nothing distinguishing. Yet."

A short nod. "Which is why I want to hold it aside and watch it."

"I... Huh. Had any other of the bruising-fever patients reported rat bites? None were mentioned to me. Rat bites seem the sort of thing people would notice."

"Not the rats," said Rede, his eyes narrowing. "Their fleas."

"Uh." Pen paused, taken aback. "That would seem to have the opposite problem. Nobody's been bitten by rats. *Everybody* is bitten by fleas." Well, not Pen. Nor anyone for a block around his house. "But not everybody has the fever. Thankfully."

"Blood. You were talking about blood being still alive once it's left the body. If you've ever managed to kill a flea that's just fed on you before the little bugger jumps away, it smears out blood. Just like a mosquito or a tick. If the blood is alive, and the contagion is alive, maybe the contagion is alive *in* the blood. At least until the flea digests it."

"That…" *is a brilliant idea*, Pen did not say aloud. It had to be flawed, somehow. "How in the world would you ever show if such a thing was so?"

"I'm not sure. How long would the blood, and the contagion in it, still be alive? Maybe a person would have to let a flea feed on a sick man, and then feed on himself." Rede's frown deepened. "It would have to be me. I couldn't ask this of anyone else."

"It most certainly could *not* be you!"

He looked up at Pen. "If I contracted the fever that way, could you save me?"

"I don't know. And that's just the first problem." How could he talk Rede out of this horrifying idea? "Anyway, it couldn't be you, or anyone else who has been up to their armpits in the sick. Because how could you tell if it was the flea bite, or your contact with the soiled linens or the vomit or the blood in the basins? It would have to be someone who was pristine with respect to this mess. Which is nobody in the whole fort, for a start. Or in the village, by now."

"Agh." Rede rubbed a weary hand over his face, shoulders slumping.

Pen sighed, hoping he'd thwarted this insane plan. "Anyway," he said after a moment. "If it really is the rats or their fleas spreading it around, new cases ought to tail off in a few days." Beguiling thought. "There being no more rats." Save this one, apparently, hidden out of the way.

"Or you've just destroyed all the evidence."

"I'd take that trade."

"No—well, yes—but…" Rede made a frustrated swipe. "Never mind."

"Have any new cases reported in here while I was gone to the village?"

"One. And the provisioner's ox-driver died."

Pen grimaced. He felt like a man treading water with no shore in sight to swim for. "I swear to all the gods, I truly don't know if I'm saving lives, or just prolonging deaths."

Rede looked at him in surprise. "Two men seemed sufficiently past the crisis that I moved them to the recovery wards."

"We have recovery wards?"

"Oh. I suppose I didn't take you in there. Yes, because we don't know whether a person can be reinfected. I try to move the ones who seem to be improving out with each other. And the ones who are better still, the same again."

Pen should have noticed. Realized. He'd been head-down among the dire cases…

"You're so pressed, I didn't think I should waste your attention upon men who are getting better, or who'd had milder cases and seem to be recovering on their own."

"Oh." *Oh, Bastard's teeth.* This was going to be just like the nightmare of Martensbridge all over again, wasn't it. Only the worst cases, *all* the worst cases, and never any easy victories. Because that would waste Pen's *time*, which was better directed toward… another worst-case. Inescapable logic. "I see."

And when had people started flowing under his hands as indistinguishably as the waters of a river? Except for those who'd died, sticking up like boulders with memory eddying around them in agitation. Pen had mainly been tracking the total of sick, the work set before him this hour, which had never gone down, only up. Had the population of their chambers turned over at least once by now? Maybe twice? Rede would know the numbers. Pen didn't ask.

A little silence, while two tired men stared at nothing much. The dark tunnel of their future, Pen supposed. "I'd best get back to it, then."

"Yes. Me as well."

But when Pen made his way out, Rede was still gazing speculatively down into his rat-box.

PENRIC, EXITING the second sick-chamber of the following morning's round and wondering if Des needed to go back to the kitchen yet, found a man waiting for him just beyond the colonnade whom he dimly recognized as one of Adelis's headquarters clerks. The fellow extended a long arm with a letter held out delicately between thumb and finger. "This came for you, Learned Penric."

"Oh. Thank you." Pen accepted it, and the clerk nodded and skittered out without waiting to take a reply; understandable. Visitors to the hospice court were as few as could be arranged at present. Master Rede had forbidden the soldiers to come see their comrades ill with the bruising fever, a prohibition that had not been hard to enforce.

Pen opened it, scattering sealing wax on the tiles, and was both pleased and disappointed to find Nikys's handwriting. He'd been hoping for some—preferably helpful—replies to his urgent notes about the contagion. But this was fine, too, since it began, *We are all well here.*

I imagine you'll first want any news from town about the sickness out at the fort. She had that right. *Gossip in the marketplace is not yet too worried—most people seem to think it's some camp dysentery or summer fever. In which case you should have been home by now. As you are not, I conclude this is something more difficult. It is, as always, useless to expect Adelis to write, so please, if you're not returning to Vilnoc today, send me some news of you. Make him write it honestly, Des!*

If the sickness has come to town, I have not yet heard of it, but that's no surprise. I expect the Mother's Order would be the first to know.

Some small household news tidbits followed, including, *We did remember to feed your sacred pets. Lin even undertook to clean their boxes,* which made Pen smirk a little. Pen kept a small menagerie of rats for magical trials—young, healthy, tame, flea-free, non-biting rats, which last Pen had assured by the application of a bit of shamanic persuasion. He'd never been able to convince their housemaid that cleaning up after them was a holy task, or even within her duties at all, but apparently Nikys, or necessity, had better luck.

At least it's not dolphins, Nikys had once sighed to Lin. His wife had wholly disapproved of Pen's shamanic experiments with the harbor dolphins, even though Pen hadn't actually drowned.

Yet, muttered Des, who'd been on Nikys's side.

Reading on: *Your correspondence is piling up. Let me know if I should bundle it up and send it out to the fort, or hold it for your return.*

Florie has been a bit fussy—Pen frowned—*but Mother says it's too early for her to be teething. So maybe she just misses you, as I do. Come home safe and soon!*

Your loving Madame Owl.

Pen vented a hopelessly fond sigh, folded the letter back up, and tucked it away inside his sash. He had a chamber full of sick men waiting. And another after that. Maybe he could write a reply during supper, which he'd have to stop for anyway.

AS HE knelt beside his first patient in the next chamber, the man's hot hand wavered up and feebly clutched Pen's, halting its blessing. "No!"

"Let me pray for you, young man."

"You aren't praying. Bastard's necromancer. You're doing some magicky thing." He scowled, fretful, feverish, and frightened. "Maybe a curse."

He wasn't the first soldier to suspect the uncanny extras, as most who didn't already know who Pen was at least realized what the silver braid in his sash meant, but he was the first to object.

"Magic, yes, a little, but I assure you, it isn't any malediction. It's an aid against the fever." Pen knew better than to promise it was a *cure*. "Come now, I treated you last night, I know, soon after you came in."

But as Pen lifted his hand, the soldier muttered incoherent protests and thrashed away, falling out of his cot, which brought the attendant orderly trotting over. He shied again as Pen tried to help him up, and Pen stood back, frustrated. Was the lad a secret Quadrene, or just full of nursery tales about evil sorcerers? *Or both.*

"Try to calm him down," Pen told the orderly. "I'll come back later."

But Pen had been a subject of worried gossip and slanderous speculation in here already, he discovered when two more sick men refused his aid. He seriously considered knocking them all unconscious with that brain-trick he'd been trying on his rats at home, and treating them anyway, but that skill was…not perfected. Also, the household cat was growing finicky about eating his failures.

He knelt beside the last cot, whose occupant was beyond protest or even awareness of Pen and his magic. Pen made his ministrations quiet and brief. This one wasn't going to be a good example to point out to his chamber mates about the harmlessness of Pen's doings, Pen feared.

He needed one of their own authorities to back him up; Master Rede, probably. Pen reflected glumly that Master Orides might have had more clout than the younger physician, and maybe more old tricks tucked in his green sash for dealing with uncooperative patients. As a last resort, Pen might try dragging in Adelis, but if the soldiers were that sick and scared, even ingrained military disciplines might break down. Rede first, then.

He spotted the man he sought under the opposite colonnade by the apothecary's chamber, talking with an orderly. They both broke off as Pen clipped up, the orderly making a vague salute and heading away to his tasks. Pen hadn't yet crossed paths with Rede at his early breakfast, nor coming back from Des's feeding, either.

"Master Rede. I'm facing a mutiny among some of your patients. Mostly I suspect due to sheer ignorance on their parts, but I don't think they'll accept tutoring from me. You might have better—" Pen broke off, staring at the gauze bandage wrapping Rede's left arm; his hand shot out to grasp his wrist and turn it over. "*What* have you done?"

Des's Sight answered his question even as he asked it. The skin beneath the gauze was sprinkled with an array of tiny inflamed dots, recognizably flea bites. "I told you not to do that!"

Rede shrugged away. "It was then or never. The rat died the next hour."

"It should have been *never*. Sunder it! I *knew* I should have killed that thing on the spot last night. *And* the fleas that rode in on it." Upset, Pen pulled Rede's other arm out, searching for wounds. "Did you make it bite you as well?"

Rede brushed him off, grimacing. "We already have one man bitten by that rat. I've set him in a chamber apart, although he didn't want to stay here. We didn't need a second example, and besides, this way I might tell whether it was the rat or its fleas."

Too late, Pen groaned inwardly. Brave, determined, desperate, deprived of sleep—no wonder Rede wasn't thinking clearly. It was a miracle—maybe?—that he wasn't down sick already, one way or another.

I don't sense any godly residue, Des answered literally the question Pen hadn't actually asked her.

Agh.

Keep an eye on those bites seemed a stupid thing to say, since no doubt Rede would be observing them obsessively. "Come find me at once if they appear to be doing anything that ordinary flea bites would not," said Pen instead.

"Of course," said Rede, in far too careless a tone for Pen's liking.

A bustle at the courtyard gate drew both their attentions.

One soldier supported another, limping. Two more were being transported on army stretchers, poles gripped on each end by bearers. Far too much blood was splashed around on the wrong sides of their skins. Pen was disturbed to recognize a couple of the Rusylli camp's guards he'd spoken with the other day.

"What's all this?" said Rede as he hurried up. "A fight?" He glanced beyond the gate, but no further parade of injured men followed.

The answer came from Adelis, striding in behind them. His scarred face was tight with that particular flavor of fury that masked furious worry.

"It was the Rusylli. Most of the encampment rose up last night, overpowered the gate guards, and fled down the road. They passed by the village quietly in the dark, thank the gods, but did stop to steal a few horses from our pastures along the way. The most of them are still afoot, though, so my cavalry can overtake them."

"They left their house-carts?" said Pen. Well, they'd have had to.

"They left nearly everything. We'd deliberately limited their provisions to short reserves, so they can only live off the countryside. How many farmsteads they'll raid along their route before we catch up will depend on how fast we move. They're heading up into the western hills, as nearly as we can make out."

Wild, rugged country; hard to live in, easy to hide in. Pen said uncertainly, "If they have their women, children, and old with them, surely they couldn't put up much of a fight?"

"Ha. You've never watched the Rusylli women, children, and old cutting the throats of enemies wounded on a battlefield. They creep over the ground like murderous gleaners picking up fallen grains. Penric—*what* did you say to those people day before yesterday?"

"Me!"

"They're not fleeing their captivity. They were largely reconciled to that. They're fleeing this bruising fever, their blue witch. More afraid of it than they are of me, which I'm going to have to teach them is an error."

"I didn't say that much," Pen protested, "apart from a bare description of the disease to find out if they recognized it. I suppose they could have picked up some marketplace gossip from the village—I know you let a few of them go in for supplies. Or from the gate guards, who do talk to them, to while away the hours if nothing else." Rybi's lover, or seducer, had been such a gate guard, Pen recalled. "And I know their children sneak away to play with the village children, who sneak away to play with them. Who knows how lurid their chatter was."

Adelis's lips tightened in vexation at these likelihoods.

It seemed doubtful that these rag-tag Rusylli could cross two entire realms and succeed in reaching the Uteny River, but the trail of bloodshed and destruction they'd leave while recklessly trying was horrible to contemplate. As much as Pen sympathized with their fears, he sympathized more with the hapless Orban farmer families who'd be caught in their path. Worse, they already might be carrying the disease with them, spreading it as they traveled; more lethal to more people, ultimately, than their warriors.

To be honest, murmured Des, *that's just as likely to come from Adelis's troop.*

No better.

Aye.

A couple of alert orderlies had arrived during this exchange. Rede motioned the whole lot of them toward his treatment rooms, but then wheeled back to Adelis.

"General Arisaydia. Especially if we're going to need more sick-chambers for wounded, I'm thinking we could shift all the fever convalescent to one of the barracks, if it could be cleared out for them."

Pen blinked. *We've treated a whole barracks' worth of patients so far…?* That was upwards of a hundred men. No wonder everyone was exhausted.

Adelis, listening, made a motion of assent. "You have that many recovering? Good. See my second. The barracks closest to the hospice would be best, I suppose."

"Yes, please." Rede made a hasty salute and hurried after the injured men.

Adelis's irritated gaze fell on Pen. "Riding out after Rusylli had not been in my plans for today, but here we are. Do you think your translation skills, or, er, other skills, might help convince them to surrender?"

Pen threw up his hands. "You have other translators. You don't have other sorcerers." At least unless someone from his Order answered his pleas for help. Maybe he should dispatch more notes. More strongly worded. "If I'm *here*, doing *this*, I can't be *there*, doing *that*. Pick one, Adelis!"

Adelis snorted out his breath through his nose, in his version of concession. "…Stay here."

He exited the gate, the aide at his heels already taking orders for the cavalry expedition.

Pen turned back toward the sick-chambers.

The Physicians of VILNOC

IN THE late afternoon, Pen plodded uphill from his rounds in the village, mulling. In the very extended family of tanners, another man and a woman had fallen sick. One household had refused Pen entry. The little boy and his mother were still alive. The younger carter seemed on the mend, but his elder brother was worse—could Pen come back tonight? He glanced up at the fort gates to find himself following a sedan chair across the drawbridge, its bearers wearing the green tunics of servants to the Mother's Order in Vilnoc.

Pen sped his steps, catching up as the bearers set the chair down in the middle of the hospice courtyard and helped its occupant clamber from the wicker seat. Doffing her wide-brimmed hat, she tossed it onto the cushion. She was a slight, aging woman in a simple tunic dress, but belted with the green sash of a senior physician. Pen's heart lifted in hope. Had someone sent them help?

Rede appeared from the door of a treatment room, wiping his hands on a cloth, and his lips parted in what Pen guessed was the same hope. He hurried out to the chair. Pen's quick glance by Sight at his left arm showed the flea bites under the now-grubby wrappings healing at about the usual rate for flea bites, for what that was worth.

The woman clutched what Pen recognized as one of his notes from…however many days ago that had been. Not a speedy response, but definitely something. At last.

Turning, she took in his summer vestments. "Ah, you are Learned Penric?" She waved the note.

"Yes, Master—?"

"Tolga."

"And this is Master Rede Licata, senior physician in this fort."

She gave Rede a solemn nod. "I'd heard about Master Orides. He was a fine physician and a good man. I am so sorry."

"As are we all, ma'am." The two healers eyed each other with professional interest, evaluating.

Rede evidently passed her muster, for she nodded again and turned to Pen. "We received your letter. What we think might be the first case of your bruising fever turned up on our doorstep this morning. I've come out to see your patients for a comparison."

Faint disappointment crossed Rede's features, but he murmured, "Of course," and gestured toward the sick-chambers. "We have, unfortunately, plenty of examples for you to look at."

This was not a tour Pen needed to take. "Des and I must pay a visit to the kitchens," he told Rede. "I shouldn't be long."

"Right."

As he strode off, he heard Tolga saying to Rede, "So what exactly is this sorcerer *doing* for your men?" and Rede replying, "Well, let me show you…"

His routine in the killing room having become practiced and efficient—chickens again—Pen returned to find the pair of them emerged from their inspection and perched on one of the stone benches in the shade of the colonnade, talking with a serious air. Rede saw him and motioned him over, shifting to give him room to sit.

Pen sank down with a tired breath, eyeing the Mother's woman across Rede. "Can your Order send us any help out here?"

She shook her head in polite regret. "In fact, I'm hoping I might take you back with me to look at our case."

Rede sat up, frowning. "We have all he can do right here. You have one"—he waved at his row of sick-chambers—"we have forty-eight."

It had been forty-seven a while ago…

"Plus however many in the village," Rede continued.

"Two more today," said Pen.

Tolga grimaced. "I'm not naïve enough to think our first case will be our last, and neither are you."

All the more reason, Rede's expression suggested, though he bit back saying so aloud. "In any event, General Arisaydia called him out to the fort. Only the general can release him, and he's not here right now."

Tolga turned more directly to the pair of them. "I'm sure that is not so. As a divine, his own Order must have his first allegiance. A senior sorcerer, even more so—they go where they will, I've heard."

"That," said Pen, "is more-or-less true, yes. And I came here." Leaving the conclusion to her. But… *town.* The menace was now inside Vilnoc's walls, it seemed, with Nikys and Florina and the rest of Pen's little household.

"I could lend you my chair. Or send one for you."

That was nearly tempting. In a sedan chair, he might doze on the way, getting double use out of the time. But Pen shook his head. "I can borrow a horse from the fort. It would be faster."

"You're going?" said Rede uneasily.

"I think I better had. To be sure what's going on."

"Only so long as you come *back*."

Pen rested his elbows on his knees, and his forehead in his linked hands. "Even with all my magics, I can't be in two places at once. If we could scare up another Temple sorcerer, *any* Temple sorcerer with a reasonably well-tamed demon, I'm sure I could train him or her in this one basic technique in a few hours." He frowned at his feet, adding with muted vehemence, "Even a *hedge* sorcerer."

Tolga asked, "Have you heard from any?"

"Not so far." Pen sat up. "I sent out letters at the same time I sent yours. Orbas is not all that rich in Temple sorcerers—there were more at my old chapterhouse back in the cantons, for all that its archdivineship wasn't a quarter the size of this duchy. Are there any stray mages you know of that I don't?"

"I don't see how I would," said Tolga, looking at him askance. And…covetously? "My Order isn't hiding any away. We don't even have a petty saint right now."

"More's the pity."

"Aye," she agreed ruefully. Her chin lifted in determination. "You'll come today?" she urged.

"Yes," Pen reluctantly promised. "I have a round of treatments to complete here, and then I should wash up before I start out. But I'll ride in before nightfall."

She gave a sharp nod of acceptance, and victory. Rede's shoulders slumped.

"I must away, then, and carry the word back to town." She rose and motioned her bearers, who'd been sitting warily in the scant shade of their vehicle, as far as they could get in all directions from the hospice colonnades. They jumped to their feet, as ready to be gone from here as their mistress, if for other reasons.

The green-sashed physician swayed out by the gate she'd entered. Pen and Rede still sat.

Watching her go, Rede asked, "Why are there so few Temple sorcerer-physicians?" His brows tightened in fresh mystification. "It's becoming plain to me how valuable you can be. I'd think the Mother's Order would be set on making as many more as possible."

"And so it is, but candidates don't grow on trees. Though they do have to be grown, even more slowly than trees." Pen considered how best to explain this. "It takes at least one full generation, sometimes more, to tame a wild-caught demon to be fit for the task. Which is done by yoking it with a responsible Temple divine, one who can imprint or pass to it the necessary...knowledge of life, I suppose you could say, of living it well. And the recipient must be a strong-minded person, too, preferably already disciplined in the physician's arts. Medical magics include some of the most powerful and subtle skills known. Handing that knowledge off to an innately chaotic demon that could ascend and run off with its possessor's body is a very bad idea."

Rede vented a thoughtful noise, taking this in.

Pen rubbed his stiff neck. "Many Temple demons are lost along the way, through time's accidents. Some are taken back by the god. Some are spoiled by bad riders, or just unsuitable ones. Also, the transfer is tricky, since the candidate must be brought together with the old sorcerer exactly at their deathbed." *Or on a roadside...* Pen had long wondered if his pivotal encounter with the dying Learned Ruchia and her demon had been as chance-met as it had seemed at the time, though it had certainly not been arranged by the *Temple.* "As you know, people seldom die to schedule."

"So...why aren't you working for the Mother? You could be brilliant. You could help so many!"

Pen smiled grimly. "*Many* turns out to be the problem. I did try my hand at the trade, back in Martensbridge. Des thinks the problem was that I was not well supervised, the Mother's Order there being inexperienced with sorcerer-physicians."

I think the problem was that the greedy gits ran you into the ground, grumped Des. *And you refused to learn to say no, till the end.*

"In any case, I found it was not my calling, so I declined at the last to take oath to the Mother's Order."

To put it mildly, said Des, shuddering.

"That seems impossible. It's *clearly* your calling!"

"Many cases entailed many failures, especially as all the most difficult ones became funneled to me. Fine when I was credited with healing, not so when my losses outraged. You saved *her*, why not *him*? It grew wearing."

Rede made a frustrated, negating gesture. "Every physician gets that."

"To be blunt," said Pen to his sandals, "when I tried to kill myself as the only way I could see to escape, I knew it was time to find another way to serve. Or Des did. I'm good at translations, you know." Oh, gods, how had that admission escaped his teeth?

Because you are too cursed tired, Des opined. *And because this one is a* good *physician. Remember how your patients used to confess to you?*

"Sorry," Pen choked.

Rede sat back, his arguments abruptly muzzled. "Ah," he said after a moment. "That."

He wasn't baffled? *Bless him.*

Rede's gaze lifted as if to count down the row of sick-chambers. His voice took on a new diffidence. "So…how are you holding up?"

"Oh," said Pen. He straightened and waved a hasty hand. "That's no longer a hazard for me. I had fewer attachments back then." He'd still been reeling from the deaths of his mother and his beloved princess-archdivine in such close succession that year, Pen supposed at this calmer remove. His life in Orbas, his new family, held more hostages against him now, blocking that form of flight. He trusted he would not become so desperately pressed over this business that he'd come to resent that fact.

Past time to get off this subject. "How are your flea bites?"

"They itch." Rede rubbed at his arm wrapping. "If anything else is going to happen, it's likely too soon to know." He glanced across at Pen. "Can you tell?"

"No. Which is either good or, as you say, too early. Let's hope for the first, eh?"

"If I start turning purple, I'm not sure if I would be frightened or relieved. I want an *answer*, not this, this…" His fists clenched. "*Any* answer!"

"Only the true one, I daresay."

"Well, yes." He scowled across at the patient chambers, and his voice fell. "…What do we do if it doesn't stop coming?"

Pen chose to take that as a rhetorical remark, because the answer, *Then we don't stop, either*, was too appalling to voice. But Rede had the right of it. As long as they didn't know how this disease was getting around so randomly, they were fighting blind. Pen needed an Adelis-brain, all tactical.

Except not actually Adelis's, said Des, *because the man is useless in the sickroom.*

Howsoever. Pen grunted to his feet. "Maybe I'll find some new clue in town tonight."

"You *will* come back," said Rede. Question, or demand? Or fear…

"It depends on what I find there. If this thing is loose in Vilnoc, my priorities could change."

"Physicians can't choose their patients."

"Unethical, yes, I know. Between Amberein and Helvia and me, I've had the training three times. But I've never taken the oath to the Mother's Order, and I've never been sorry. Apologetic, maybe, but that isn't the same." The white god's more, ah, *fluid* approach to bestowing tasks upon Pen and his resident demon suited him better, despite its occasional seeming-lunacy.

...But was this one of them? He was ironically betrayed, if so.

Rede's mouth opened, and shut, on some further protest. "Let's hope you can learn something new in Vilnoc, then."

"Aye."

IT WAS almost sunset by the time Pen rode the army plodder he'd been lent through Vilnoc's western gate. The main chapterhouse and hospice of the Mother's Order lay at the opposite end of town, and he looked around as he threaded his way through the winding streets. Nothing seemed amiss, residents drawing in to their homes for the night in the usual rhythm. He passed the corner of his own street, and shuddered with longing to be one of those contented residents. *No.*

The main marketplace was almost deserted, the last few vendors giving up and taking in their wares, apart from a few horses and mules tethered for the night at the far end devoted to livestock sales, heads down munching desultorily at a wispy drift of hay. One nickered in curiosity at Pen's horse, who returned the greeting. Competing for their fodder, their unsuccessful owner was setting up his bedroll on a hay pile, ready to try again in the morning. A couple of other men camped to guard their more bulky goods, such as the large stack of ceramic storage jars.

Around a few more corners and small squares, up a slope, and the Mother's Order hove into Pen's view. The Vilnoc chapterhouse was an old merchant's mansion bequeathed in someone's will a generation ago, and its hospice the former warehouse, gradually refitted to its new purpose. Penric had not been inside before, his own household having no need to call on its services.

At the gate, he found the porter just raising the oil lantern that would burn all night over the open doorway. He recognized and respectfully saluted

Pen's vestments—new-laundered, but more frayed with every day of this crisis, like their wearer—took charge of Pen's horse, and directed him on to Master Tolga's lair.

He found the Mother's physician in a writing cabinet she shared with several others of her Order, most of them evidently gone home for the night or to dinner—Pen's dinner had been a handful of bread and meat jerky eaten while riding in. She rose at once when he knocked on the door jamb.

"Ah! Learned! You did come!"

"I said I would."

She shrugged. "Things happen."

"Aye. Have any more things happened here?"

"Unfortunately, yes. Another feverish girl—I'll take you to see her, too, if you would be so kind."

"As long as I'm here."

She nodded and led him out onto her second-floor gallery, down, and through an archway to the former warehouse turned holy hospice. It was laid out as another colonnaded rectangle around a central court, its own well dug new and deep; just the one level, as the old merchants would not have wanted to hoist their goods up and down stairs. The big gate at the end that could admit wagons was now closed and barred. The chapterhouse's front door would remain open at all times, mark of the Order's vow to turn no one away. This resulted, naturally, in the hospice filling up with the indigent sick and injured, such that anyone who could afford it preferred to engage a physician privately to visit them at home.

Every cot in the sick-chamber was occupied by more routine residents, although the bed of Pen's prospective patient was shoved a little aside. A small barred window, pierced through the far wall as part of the conversion, let in air and, now, dusk. A dedicat lit an oil lantern hanging from a central hook, and Tolga took up a candle in a glass vase, holding it above the cot. Pen didn't bother to tell her he didn't need it to see his work, because the fellow laid out, feverish and restless, needed to see him.

A quick examination by sight and Sight told Pen that Tolga had not misdiagnosed; the tell-tale mottled flush in the man's hands and feet was starting. Luckily, he wasn't so far along that he couldn't speak or answer questions. Struggling to prop his shoulders up against the headboard, he regarded Pen with fever-blurred curiosity.

The fellow turned out to be a merchant's clerk from Trigonie, sailed into the port ten days ago with a load of mixed goods. He'd not been outside of Vilnoc's walls since, and his sickness was too recent for him to be suspected as any sort of source; he must have contracted it after he'd arrived. His master had brought him here, not unreasonably preferring not to share his inn room with a deathly ill retainer, but paying in advance for his care, good man. So, not indigent, merely very far from home and unhappy about it. The clerk's work had kept him mostly around the harbor, but he had walked all about the town to see it in his off hours.

As usual, he'd never met a sorcerer before. Though his expression betrayed bewilderment, he accepted Pen's prayers and magic, again explained merely as a help against fever, like some sort of spiritual willow-bark decoction. Pen finished with a few reassuring platitudes about the excellence of the Mother's Order in Vilnoc, which gratified both of his listeners and wasn't untrue. Pen did not promise he'd come back.

"Well," said Pen to Tolga, rising and shaking out the knees of his trousers. "Let's see your other suspect."

She guided him around to a chamber devoted to women.

The girl in the cot there, a servant much like Lin from a house in town, was very feverish and distraught. The fever had been the familiar sudden fierce onslaught. The distraction was from being turned out onto the street and told to make her own way to the hospice; summarily discharged, Pen gathered, more to save her employer the expense of her illness than to protect the rest of the family from infection. He bit back a scowl at this. She had not been outside the town walls in months, despite running errands hither and thither within them—she could not remember all the places, although the list she did give him was maddeningly long, and did not include the port.

Pen summoned all his charm for her, and also as much uphill magic as he could force her body to accept. For whichever cause, she was weakly smiling when he left. This was an early case; if he could come back for more treatments, her prognosis should be good.

Pen had hoped the new examples might offer him some clarity, but they only increased the fog. Also his worry for Nikys, but he didn't need to discuss that here. "Let's go talk somewhere," he told Tolga.

They settled on a bench by the well in the darkening courtyard, the flickering candle-vase between them.

"Was she another of the same sickness?" Tolga asked.

"Yes. Well-spotted. You should see the flushing in her extremities by tomorrow, unless my early treatment helps push it back."

Tolga nodded in a mix of satisfaction and frustration. "Exactly how is that working?"

"Have you dealt with a sorcerer-physician before?"

"Once, some years ago in the winter capital, but briefly, and I can't say as I understood what she was doing."

So, not quite as untutored as young Rede, but almost. Pen ran down the same account of the limitations and uses of his uphill magic that he'd given to the army physician, which made her frown, though not, Pen thought, from lack of understanding.

A burly male dedicat came out to draw up a couple of buckets of well water, by a clever foot-wheel mechanism which Pen would have been glad to examine. If he ever again had time.

"Do you think we can expect more of these fevered?" asked Tolga bluntly when the creaking died away.

"I truly don't know, because I still have no idea how the accursed thing is getting *around*," said

Pen. "If it follows the same pattern as in the fort and Tyno, then yes." A sprinkling, and then more, and then…

"Can you stay?"

"Of course not."

"…Can you come back?"

"I don't know. There seem to be more sick out at the fort every time I turn around." And adding in a couple of hours of travel, even if he visited the Order only once a day, would put Pen further behind schedule for all the sick he already owned. At what point would his treatments, already slipping from optimum to minimum, become so attenuated as to be useless?

Anything to add, Des? His demon had been oddly silent, not even offering tart quips. *Observations, memories?*

Nothing helpful. Carry on.

Was she growing as wearied as he was? He'd been using her hard, and more continuously than ever before. He knew better than most that *powerful* was not the same thing as *invulnerable.*

Pen continued to Tolga, "Send a message to the fort describing them if you get new cases, though. I especially want to know where people have been, what they were doing, before they contracted this." He huffed a breath. "Although I know quite a lot already, and it's not helping."

Tolga let him go with great reluctance, although she could hardly kidnap him. He could tell she was tempted, though. He didn't tell her exactly how she might accomplish it.

He remounted his horse outside the chapter-house's door and turned its head toward Vilnoc's western gate. He must write to Nikys again tonight, he decided, warning her of these new developments in town without the distortions of marketplace rumor. He'd fumigated his first note to her the other day with burning sage before he'd sent it off, but he wasn't sure that the smoke had done anything other than make the paper smell odd.

He passed his own street again with a pang. The scholar's life he had achieved with such trouble—the wife, the child, the peaceful study, the cat, the well-run modest household—could all be lost to him, he'd always known, any time he rode out for the duke or the archdivine, by some misadventure happening to *him*. He'd never pictured his refuge being stolen away from him while his back was turned, but his well-stocked imagination now supplied him with several versions of just how that could occur.

And it was not just his own immediate family at risk. Rybi and her son at the orphanage, Lencia and Seuka and the other young dedicats at his own Order's chapterhouse, all his other Temple friends there and at the curia of the archdivine, right up through Duke Jurgo's own household—in a mere three years of residence, how had he acquired such a huge array of friends vulnerable to fate in Orbas? And Adelis, well, Adelis was always at hazard by his choice of trade, but this was not any hero's death he might have imagined for himself.

Pen rode out to the fort road slowly—he could see in the dark, his horse could not—and did not turn aside.

THE NEXT three days passed in an increasing blur for Pen. He looped back and forth from the hospice to the kitchens, to Tyno, to the kitchens again, and a daily ride into town which qualified as his sole break. There, Tolga had acquired five more fevered people, none with any relation to another that Pen could determine. If there were more sick tucked away privately in their own houses, they'd not yet been brought to Pen's attention, and he wasn't going to go looking for them.

Arriving back from the most recent of these evening excursions to Vilnoc, he encountered Rede having an equally late dinner in the staff mess. Pen thought he recognized the dead-rabbit bits in the cooling hash Rede was shoving around absently with his fork. The page of scratchy notes Rede was studying was new.

Pen thunked down opposite him and tried to work up more enthusiasm for his own meal. He was hungry enough; just tired.

"Any more men arrive sick while I was in town?" Pen asked.

"Yes, two. But I moved one more man to the convalescent chamber, so he's off your list."

Two steps backward, one forward? It was still a march in the wrong direction. "What do you have there?"

"A roster of the sick, and when they arrived, stripped down to just days and numbers. Including Tyno and Vilnoc. There is something odd about the way they are progressing. It feels strange to say it, but they aren't coming fast enough."

Pen rubbed his neck. "Have you run mad? Any more, and I'll be overwhelmed." If he wasn't already.

Rede waved his worksheet in impatience. "It's just that if people were giving it directly to each other, cases should be doubling and redoubling, because that's what contagions *do*. But after the initial burst, it's settled in to a steady supply. Increasing, yes, I'm afraid so, but not…not in that way."

"I can hardly be sorry, I suppose."

"Yes, but d'you see, this suggests… I'm not sure what. That everyone is getting it from the same source?"

"In the fort, and Tyno, and Vilnoc, *and* that border town a hundred miles west?" The first three, maybe, but surely not the last. Pen glanced at Rede's left arm, where the flea bites were almost healed. "But not from rat fleas, apparently."

"You, ah, see nothing going on in me with your magical vision?"

"I have looked at, and into, so many patients by now, in every stage of this thing, I could diagnose it in my sleep." And so he was, in his more unpleasant dreams. The waking nightmare was bad enough; he didn't need the even weirder versions. "You have no incipient bruising fever. Offer your thanks to the god of fools and madmen. Which would be mine, I suppose."

"Hah."

Pen addressed his plate. "The elder carter in Tyno died this morning. Add him to your list." His wife—now widow—had been distraught, with that extra edge that hope disappointed gave. No matter how little Pen tried to promise, how briefly explain, people built up expectations of his magic that crashed down hard with its failures. Worse, he sometimes thought, than if he'd never tried at all. "His brother is getting better, though."

Rede nodded. Not patients he'd seen, touched, talked to; he could maintain his composure.

"I don't… I'm starting to wonder if I'm actually doing anything, or just deluding myself." And everyone else.

Rede tapped his notes. "Oh. That's really interesting, too. Among the first wave of men who came in with the bruising fever, what, three weeks ago now, one died in two. A few days after Adelis brought you, that dropped to one in five. Now, one in ten. With occasional setbacks. I'm certain that improvement is your doing."

"That's...not good enough. My uphill magic is getting stretched too thinly. Even you will be able to tell within a couple more days, because that mortality will start to rise again. I *can't* work any faster." He glanced up at Rede. "When that moment comes, *you* have to choose which people I will keep treating and which I will abandon. I won't be able to." Would Rede put his soldiers first, as Adelis had wanted? It was where his sworn loyalty lay, after all.

"I..." Rede scraped his hand through his scalp, ducked his head, grimaced. "All right."

Army men. Pen wasn't sure whether to be grateful or horrified.

Doesn't matter. He washed down his hash with a not-very-watered beaker of fort wine, and pushed off to the sick-chambers.

PENRIC MADE his way back from the kitchens the following afternoon—late, he was always late these days—wondering whether it would be more efficient to go down for his rounds in Tyno before he washed up and rode into Vilnoc, or after. Crossing the entry court inside the fort's front gate, he was stopped short by the sight of a new and unexpected figure.

The old man standing with his old horse's reins twisted around his arm, talking with a gate guard, wore a road-grimy, home-cut version of Bastard's summer whites, lacking decorative embroidery. A tarnished metallic braid circling the tunic's standing collar stood in for the formal torc. The silver braid in his sash was merely cheap gray cloth, but the demon inside him, much younger than himself, was entirely genuine.

"Bastard bless us," breathed Pen, and strode toward them in fragile hope.

The fellow looked to be on the high side of sixty. Likely stouter when younger, much like his bony farm horse; his skin had grown loose with age, wrinkling. In coloration, he was of the Cedonian type, but hewn from a lighter wood, like fresh oak. His hair was cut in a military style overdue for scissors. Once black, it was gray with white streaks that reminded Pen of fog over thawing snow.

The gate guard looked over, and said, "Oh, there he is now."

The visitor followed his glance to Pen, and his gray eyebrows climbed. He started to step eagerly forward; the young demon within him recoiled in fright at the dense presence of Des, resulting in a sidewise trip, till he frowned sternly and righted himself. "None of that, now. Behave yourself," he muttered.

The demon settled like a dog cowering before a stern master, and no wonder; it had been a dog, or rather been in a dog, at one time, Pen was certain. The new-hatched elemental had found its early way through lesser animals before that, maybe, but mostly it was doggish. This man was clearly its first human rider, Temple-approved and with luck trained by the white god's Order. And if he wasn't, he was about to be…

The other sorcerer looked up at Pen and blinked in surprise. "You are really Learned Penric of Martensbridge? And Lodi? I was expecting someone older." He waved a familiar note clutched in his free hand, which explained his presence, but not his form of address. Pen had signed his urgent missives *Learned Penric of Vilnoc.*

"I was at one time, but I owe allegiance to the archdivine of Orbas, now. Via the Bastard's chapterhouse in Vilnoc." The functionaries there paid his stipend, anyway. "And you would be…?"

"Oh. Learned Dubro from the town of Izbetsia. Although I'm afraid I'm not very learned, by your standards." He gave a self-deprecating and somewhat nervous chuckle. "I was Brother Dubro there for years, a dedicat serving the Son of Autumn." He gestured a tally sign, ending with his hand spread over his heart. "But then there was this demon, which forced many unexpected changes in my life." He tapped his lips apologetically.

"Yes, they do that," agreed Pen. "If you'd pledged yourself to Autumn, how did the white god's Order come to gift you with a demon?"

"It was the other way around. I acquired my demon more-or-less by accident, and the Temple decided I should keep it."

"Ah. Sorcerers are made that way more often than is commonly realized. I shall like to hear more about that, later. But I see you have one of my letters about the bruising fever?"

"Yes, the Vilnoc chapterhouse forwarded it to me in Izbetsia. But did you really want help from just any sorcerer? Because I have no physician's training at all."

"I can remedy that," said Pen fervently. "You came. That's the only qualification needed."

He nodded in uncertainty, still staring in some wonder at Pen. Though not in doubt; he could sense Desdemona as readily as Pen could sense his doggish passenger.

Pen directed the gate guard to offload the saddlebags and stable Dubro's horse. A polite contest over who was going to carry the bags was won by their owner. Pen led his welcome guest through the fort to the hospice.

"I'm bunking in with the orderlies," Pen told him. Maybe not a good moment to mention that some had come down sick with the fever themselves? Pen didn't want to scare this godly gift away. "We'll find you a spare cot. Try not to wake up anyone who's sleeping—they probably have night duty."

Pen had Dubro set his bags on Pen's bed before following him to the courtyard fountain for a washup.

"How far a ride is it from Izbetsia?" Pen asked, eyeing his travel dirt. He suspected he'd have to look at one of Adelis's larger-scale maps to find the town marked.

"Two days, at the best speed my old horse and I go," said Dubro, scrubbing industriously.

"You came quickly?"

"After I got the note I took a day to think about it. And to pray."

"It is a frightening disease."

"Oh, that's not it." He waved a negating hand, also shaking the water off. His splashes evaporated from the sun-heated tiles. "But I wasn't sure we could be of use."

"It's a very young demon to be set to such a task, though I've been thinking about how to make it as straightforward as possible. Let's go find out."

"Right now?" He straightened, startled.

"Oh, yes."

For all his claim to bravery, Dubro did hesitate at the door of the first sick-chamber, but gulped and followed Pen into the dimness and stink. Pen wondered if he should have diverted for some medical lecture first, but really, this was going to be easier to show than describe. He picked a soldier who was too woozy with fever to complain or comment, and had the older sorcerer kneel alongside him.

"Just watch, for the first few."

Pen had dispensed with the disguising prayers a few beleaguered days ago, but he did make a salute of a tally sign before commencing the first application of uphill magic. Dubro squinted his eyes in concentration, though following this with inner more than outer vision.

"I've only worked with downhill magics, before," he murmured. "Small and safe."

"Not unwise, if you've had no mentor. Er, have you been all on your own in Izbetsia?"

"We've a senior Temple divine who is my supervisor, but he trained with the Father's Order. It's not a big town."

Supervisor, or wary watchman? Pen would wager the latter. So likely not an encourager of experimentation or exploration. Pen could see how being made responsible for something one could neither understand nor control could make one a touch rigid, even without the typical tidy-mindedness of those attracted to the Father of Winter's service.

You are too charitable, Pen, reproved Des. *If this fellow has had his dog for as long as it looks, it's been a waste of opportunity.*

Dubro's glance shifted aside. He wouldn't be able to make out Des's silent speech, but that she spoke, he sensed.

I don't imagine the dog's been very chatty, she added.

Ha. Unlike the ten of you…

My first human rider Sugane found the speechless imprints of the mare and the lioness extremely confusing, I'll grant. But back then she had no Temple support at all. This Orban country man seems luckier.

Pen worked his way all around the six patients in the chamber, then led Dubro out again.

"And now, on to the kitchens."

"The kitchens? I admit, I'm a little peckish."

"We'll get to eat in the orderlies' mess, later on," Pen assured him. "But I have an arrangement with the cooks for dumping Des's chaos, which I'll demonstrate shortly. Also, I didn't think your first trials with transferring uphill magic should be on people."

His brow wrinkled. "All right…"

"Follow me."

Dubro chuckled as they exited the hospice court. "I already know my way around this fort, or rather, it's coming back to me. I served here, oh…over forty years ago, because I remember the celebration when young Duke Jurgo was born."

The duke was now a hale man in his mid-forties, so that dated it with precision. "You were in the Orban army?"

"Aye. I joined at age sixteen, all young and hot—I couldn't wait to get out of my home village. Funny, after my twenty years, I couldn't wait to go home. I took my veteran's allotment of land as close to my birthplace as I could get it, outside Izbetsia. Married a widow I'd known as a girl, had two youngsters of my own before her womb closed up—that was a good time. They're both grown now. I helped out with the town temple on holy days as a lay dedicat."

"You didn't have your demon then?"

"No, that came later. As a surprise all around. I had a good old farm dog, Maska. One night he killed a weasel that was trying to get at our hens. We figured out much later that the weasel had picked up a demon elemental from a wild bird it had killed, probably a quail. I thought for a while the dog had run mad, or fallen sick, and I was going to have to put him out of his misery, but after a week or two he settled back down. He was never quite the same, after, but he was still loyal to me."

By which Pen concluded that the distressed Dubro had been putting off that unpleasant duty to which, as either soldier or farmer, he should have been steeled. Also that the stronger personality of the dog had overcome the influence of both the demon and its prior animal possessors, which was unusual and most interesting, theologically speaking.

"I kept old Maska for over a year after that, till he died of a tumor. In my arms. And then I got the demonic surprise. It gave me the cold grue later to realize he might just have likely died with my wife or my youngsters, and given the demon to one of them. My wife thought *I* had run mad and sick, maybe over grief for the dog, and I was wondering myself."

Pen put in, "My demon, at least, had been in several humans before, and could explain itself." *At great length.*

Now, now, murmured Des in amusement, as fascinated by this tale as Pen.

"Ah? That would have helped a good deal, aye. It wasn't till our divine took me to a Temple sensitive in Vilnoc that I was rightly diagnosed. They sent me on to Trigonie, where there was a special saint who was supposed to have the gift of removing demons, but after looking me over she decided instead I should keep my demon and tame it for the Temple. They swore me to the white god's service and held me there for a year, training me up as a divine of sorts. I wasn't very happy about it at the time, but as I behaved myself and did what they told me to, they did let me go back to my farm."

"Have you farmed there ever since?"

"Aye. My wife left me for a while out of fear, but she came back, good old girl. She passed on to her goddess about four years ago. Our boy has taken over the farm for me, in the main."

"I see."

They came to the delivery entrance to the killing room, and Pen ushered Dubro inside. His demon was still very wary of Des, so there was a brief tussle between Dubro getting close enough to his new mentor to hear and see, and his demon trying to get as far away across the room as possible. Dubro won. Des controlled her natural irritation smoothly.

The lads had saved Pen out a crate of chickens for emergency night rations, as was become routine.

"You say you've worked downhill magics? Killing vermin, fleas and rats and the like?"

"Yes, I did learn to do that, early on."

"Poultry for the table?"

"Not so much. I taught Maska *firmly* as a pup not to worry the chickens, so he gets edgy over that. I just kill them in the usual way, at home."

"You think of your demon as Maska? You've named him?" Pen smiled in approval.

"Keeping his old name seemed easiest. Eh, does your demon have a name? Or names?"

"Eleven of them, one each for her prior human riders, and one I gave her for all of her together. Desdemona, or Des for short. Naming your demon is a very useful thing. A lot of sorcerers don't figure that out, so good for you."

"Huh." He stared at Pen. Or through Pen at Des, maybe. "It—she?—is so dense and deep. Yet she doesn't ascend? You aren't afraid?"

"We, ah, came to an understanding early on, so no." Pen turned back to their more immediate problems. "Divesting the excess chaos that will accrue to your demon from the, as it were, uphill donations to the sick men will be exactly the same as killing vermin, directed to precise targets, so I don't have to teach you that part." *Thanks be.* "Right now, I want you to try placing a bit of the uphill magic just as I showed you in the sick-chamber, but into a chicken."

"Ah, I get it." Dubro opened the crate and expertly removed one chicken. He stroked its feathers, frowned, and concentrated. The blast of uphill magic was well-directed, at least. The chicken squawked, flapped its wings wildly, and, as nearly as Pen could tell, died of a heart attack.

"Oh," said Dubro, daunted. "That wasn't good." Gingerly, he set down the feathered corpse, which stopped twitching after a few more moments.

"Actually, it wasn't bad. Just too much at once. Also, still too much to try to put into a sick person at one go. You had the right move. Now let's work on finer control."

Three more chickens died before Dubro caught the trick of it, but then he did, in that odd sudden way so familiar to Pen of breaking through to a new skill. He didn't quite seem to believe Pen's praise, but they worked through the rest of the crate, saving a couple of fowls at the end for Dubro to practice divesting the accumulated disorder, after calming Maska's inhibitions.

Pen ruthlessly slaughtered the survivors, because he next had to walk down to Tyno. Or, at this hour, jog down to Tyno. This left two sorcerers sitting on the stained flagstones surrounded by a dozen dead chickens, and Dubro shaking his head.

"Is this really going to work?"

"Yes," said Pen firmly, because confidence was important in dealing with demons. And humans. He scrambled to his feet and helped the older man up. After shouting into the kitchen for the lads to come collect their next plucking job, news not received with joy, Pen led back to the hospice.

"Will it be all right with the Temple authorities for me to be doing this kind of magic?" asked Dubro in lingering doubt. That first chicken had unnerved him, Pen thought.

"I'm the senior Temple authority for sorcery in Vilnoc, so yes."

Dubro's lips twitched. "Aye, I've known officers like that…"

"Just wait till you meet Adelis. Uh, General Arisaydia."

"That will be a marvel." He nodded without irony.

In the ensuing patient chamber, Pen picked a less badly off soldier for Dubro to try. Were their two magics going to prove compatible? Or should Pen work up separate rosters for each of them?

Separate if you can, advised Des. *I could handle it, but that dog has enough new things on his plate.*

Leaving Pen to assign himself the worst cases; it was obvious enough how this had to go. Again.

The sick soldier eyed the elderly sorcerer with more confidence than he usually bestowed on youthful-seeming Penric; Pen did not try to correct this misapprehension. Dubro knelt, gulped, prayed—more for himself than for his patient, Pen suspected—pressed his spread hand to the fevered chest, and let a dose of magic flow.

"Very good. Stop."

He hauled Dubro back out to the courtyard, where he blinked in the too-westering sunlight, shaken. His demon was a little twitchy with the new demand and the inflow of disorder, but not at all out of control.

"That was perfect," Pen told him. Or close enough. "While that's settling in, let's go get Master Rede and introduce you. Senior fort physician. He runs the show in the hospice. It's been a hard month for him, but you'll find him a good man."

While Pen *wanted* to toss Dubro straight into the bottomless pool of need, here, it would be a very bad idea. Young demons were very vulnerable to mishandling. The little time spent training would be repaid later.

They found Rede in a treatment chamber just finishing setting a soldier's broken arm, because life went on in the fort. The majority of its denizens remained unaffected by the bruising fever except by fear, thank the gods, and *why?* The pattern of those who hadn't contracted it was as mysterious as that of those who had.

Rede sent the soldier off with his arm in a sling and instructions to rest, and turned to his new callers. His tired face lit when Pen introduced Learned Dubro and explained why and how he'd come.

"I've just acquainted him with his medical duties. I'll leave you to get him settled in. He's had a long ride today, with a pretty abrupt tutorial at the end, and hasn't had dinner yet." He eyed Rede. "Have you had a break?"

Rede stared blankly, as if Pen had spoken in Darthacan. After a moment he offered, "Funerals. I went to some."

"So no, I see. I have to run down to Tyno." Literally, if he wanted to be back before darkness fell. "Then Vilnoc." For the best result, he should be visiting each patient more than once a day. Maybe Dubro could make the difference?

"Any more cases down there?"

"I'll find out soon. Learned Dubro has some interesting stories to tell. And he should hear all you've learned about this disease he'll be helping treat. I'll see you both when I get back." Pen strode out, waving without turning around.

PENRIC RETURNED to the fort from Vilnoc long after dark, to find Rede and Dubro talking earnestly in the lamplight of Rede's writing cabinet.

"Oh, good, you're back." Rede seemed to greet Pen's every return with relief, as if in fear Pen might abscond somewhere, or more likely be abducted and held prisoner by the Mother's Order. Pen imagined Tolga had thought about it. "What's new to report?"

Pen swallowed his last bite of probably-ox jerky—it had lasted his whole ride—and answered, "Three new cases in the village. One in town. No one else died this afternoon. Although a couple of people at the Order are in a bad way. I'd like to see them twice tomorrow if I can." Actually, he'd *like* to see them three times, or maybe four. More than four treatments in a day, he'd discovered in his prior career, were in general too much for the patient to absorb, and so the effort was wasted. Three or four were ideal, but he wasn't going to be able to do that many, so there was no use brooding about it. Or rather, it had been out of the question before Dubro's arrival. Pen's arithmetic might be about to improve. He smiled at the other sorcerer in much the hungry way that Rede and Tolga smiled at him. Dubro smiled back in uncertainty.

Pen's eye fell upon an unexpectedly familiar slim codex open on Rede's table between the two men. It was Pen's own translation into Adriac of Learned Ruchia's primer on the basics of sorcery, printed three years ago in Lodi by the archdivine's press. "Oh! However did you come by that?"

"Ah, so you *did* write it?" said Dubro. "I thought you must be the same man, but then I thought you were too young. It was sent to me last year by a friend in the Trigonie Temple."

"You read Adriac, then?" Pen asked, pleased.

Dubro shook his head in regret. "No. Our town divine reads a little, and helped me go over it, but I don't really think he understood the sorcery parts."

"Which would be…pretty much all of it, oh dear."

"Even so, I could see it was clearer and plainer than some of what I'd been taught when I first got Maska." Dubro tapped the open page.

"Yes, Learned Ruchia was very good. It was the first volume that ever fell into my hands about my craft, and still the best, so I was lucky."

Dubro frowned. "She still lives on in your head, doesn't she?"

"Her imprint, yes, that was very helpful, too. Although she can get tart with me when I'm slow. When I first ran across her book back in Martensbridge, written in our native Wealdean, it only existed in a few manuscript copies, horrifyingly rare and vulnerable. One of my first tasks as a young divine was to transcribe it for printing. Oh, making printing plates by sorcery—I'll wager that's another skill I could teach you. Although not this week."

"Ho, I saw that in the codicil."

"Yes, that part I really did write. Since I made up the technique."

Intent, Rede asked, "Is it true there's supposed to be a second volume about medical sorcery?"

"Yes!" said Pen happily. "I finally finished making all the wooden plates and shipped them off to the archdivine of Adria last fall. The book is three times as thick as this one, in both senses, so it took a while. Completing Volume Two for him was part of the bargain I'd struck for releasing me to the service of Orbas, when I moved here. I very much wanted to finish it anyway, so it was an easy promise to make. They're supposed to send me copies soon. I hope."

"I see."

"Do you read Adriac?" Pen inquired in hope.

"Ah, not well. I have better Roknari—army men tend to learn the languages of their enemies. But there is not likely to be a work on medical sorcery in that tongue."

"You'd be surprised what gets handed around in secret. But no, the Roknari writings I've read on sorcery were odd and obscure, by Ruchia's strict standards. Partly to hide what they were writing, which…rather defeats the purpose of writing, partly I think because their understanding was distorted by Quadrene theological teachings." Pen could go on at length on the topic, but now was not the time.

Dubro said tentatively, "But will there ever be a translation to Cedonian? That I could read, maybe?"

Pen gave a vigorous nod. "I've been working on one under the patronage of Duke Jurgo. Revising as I go, since every time I've translated it, it seems I've learned more. It keeps getting longer, so, slower."

You're going to have to put your name on it as a co-writer, if this keeps up, said Des, smug. Or was that Ruchia? Someone in his head was pleased with his progress, anyway. After the Wealdean, the Darthacan, and the Adriac translations, Des usually just complained about the tedium of sitting through it all *again*.

"How many times have you translated it?" asked Dubro, staring at him.

"Uh, four? Counting the Wealdean in as one. Four and a half with the Ibran, but that was interrupted before I'd got very far. I want to get back to it someday."

"I'd like to see that second volume in Cedonian," said Rede.

"I'd love to have you do so. The first draft needs checking by someone well-up in current Cedonian medical usage. Before I recopy it for the printing plates. I'm hoping to be able to use metal plates for Jurgo's edition—I'm working with his court printer on that. More durable than wood, able to make many more copies before wearing out."

Rede and Pen gazed at each other in a moment of mutual rapacity, before Rede sighed and said, "After this is over."

"Aye." Pen stretched, preparatory to the effort of standing. Up. Again.

Rede fingered the volume, a thoughtful look on his features, then gently closed it. "This could be quite important. Instead of sharing your knowledge with one apprentice at a time, you might reach hundreds. Perhaps people you'll never even meet."

"That's my hope, anyway. Why I crouch over my writing table for months on end."

Fibster, murmured Des. *You love your writing table.*

More than he loved this nightmare in which he was presently embedded, to be sure. But maybe, now, not alone? "Ready for another trial in the sick-chambers?" he asked Dubro.

Dubro gulped, ducked his head in assent, and followed him to his feet.

Rede went along to watch them work their way through the next chamber full of men. Frustrating for him, since there was nothing for normal human eyes to see but a mismatched pair of Temple-men kneeling by cots, moving their hands a bit and conversing in low tones. Dubro and his dog perceived much more. The rural divine might have come late in life to being a lettered man, but Pen doubted he'd ever been a dull one.

By the time Pen led back to the kitchens for the midnight slaughter, he was hoping he might leave Dubro to work unsupervised as early as tomorrow afternoon. Which was insanely faster than any normal tutorial, but this wasn't a normal situation. The Trigonie saint seemed to have judged the supplicant sorcerer's strength of character correctly, back at his beginning.

Or her Master did, said Des.

Let's pray so.

PENRIC DIDN'T know whether it was the former disciplines as a soldier or as a farmer that had fitted Dubro for his new challenge. Both involved relentless routines dutifully carried out, daily without a break, the latter even more than the former. Keeping animals and plants alive and healthy, not to mention children, year in and year out, was certainly a more complex task than garrison guard.

Howsoever Dubro had been prepared, by noon the next day Pen thought him ready to try a roster of patients under Rede's eye, including the fellows who had recently resisted Pen's sorcery. To Pen's dark amusement, Dubro's local origins and reassuring age, grandfather laced with sergeant, seemed to overbear the soldiers' prior superstitious fears, although the fact that they were growing sicker and less able to object doubtless played in.

The young demon Maska was a keener concern, but his inherited canine loyalty to his—evidently once equally loving—master granted an edge over his underlying chaotic demon-nature. The skill Pen taught was an advanced technique, but it was only the one, and by the time anyone had repeated a task that often, that close in succession, growing adept was almost an inevitability. Demons, Pen knew too well, tended to become bored and cranky with repetition, but there appeared to be no end to the number of times a dog delighted in fetching a stick.

Pen watched until he felt confident he could let the pair get on with it, then cantered off to Tyno and Vilnoc and his other two rosters of patients for the first, but not the only, *ha*, visit of the day.

Meanwhile, Pen had a demon nearer than Maska to concern him. By the time he rode back from Vilnoc, where in his relief and hope he'd poured all the uphill magic he could muster into Tolga's now-ten patients, following directly from Tyno's now-seventeen, Pen's tunic was dank with sweat and Des was mute, brimming with unshed chaos. And it wasn't the good sort of silence from her.

Pen diverted his horse around the fort's down-wind side to the slope where its abattoir was situated. The small building had its own aqueduct branch running into it, used in keeping the pavement rinsed in its dismembering courtyard, but the initial killing, skinning, and quartering of the large animals was done in a yard outside, cluttered with hoists, cranes, chutes and carts. The reek that rose from it was intense, and Pen's horse snorted and shied.

Pen had participated in butchery in his own rural youth, on the farm at Jurald Court and on hunts, but the cantons were much colder than Orbas. This was a rare moment for Pen to appreciate that. The fort butchers wasted very little of their animals, but the residue of offal raked off to the side still made an unsavory daily banquet for crows, ravens, stray dogs, and flies. Pen decanted a splash of chaos upon the flies on his way in, like a libation spilled from an overflowing drinking vessel, but it wasn't going to be enough.

A small shrine to the Son of Autumn was set up at the side of the killing yard, in mindful gratitude for His creatures sacrificed here. The sergeant in charge no doubt led his men in a brief prayer before it as they commenced each day's work, mitigating the unavoidable brutality. As a usually unthinking beneficiary of their labors, Pen was heartened at the vision.

He sought out the workmen, finding them inside with a lot of very sharp tools turning an ex-ox into cutlets. Sergeant Jasenik proved a stringy old buzzard, an Orban army veteran cut from the same cloth as the fort cook Burae. Since a couple of his own men had come down with the bruising fever and passed into Pen's care, his anxious interest in their fates overcame whatever fears of sorcery he might have harbored. The rumors of Pen's activities in the fort hospice and kitchen had already come to his ears, if garbled, so Pen's explanations didn't have to start from scratch, quite. Pen went into more detail about how he'd used to work with that butcher in Martensbridge, which set up a strange sort of professional camaraderie between them, or at least made Jasenik decide Pen wasn't just a typical town-bred fool.

"We do most of our killing in the morning," the sergeant told Pen, to no surprise. "But there's one pig still left today."

"That would certainly do. I can only handle one large animal at a time."

"Ho. We're the same, so maybe we can match up all right."

He rounded up four of his men and led them back outside, where a surly hog waited in an enclosure. Their prayer at their shrine was more perfunctory than Pen had fondly imagined, though they seemed to appreciate him adding his own official-Temple-divine blessing. The hog did not cooperate with its doom, but after a practiced tussle the crew had it hoisted for killing.

Which Pen quietly accomplished. The screeching sensation along his nerves from the overload of chaos died away along with the animal's squeals.

Oh, wheezed Des in a profound relief that Pen frankly shared.

Everyone stepped back in surprise at the unaccustomed silence. "Is that…all right…?" asked one man.

"It died without pain," Pen promised him.

They accepted this in a hesitant sort of faith. Although they stood a little farther from him, after.

All right was a broader question, theologically speaking. Domesticated animals were considered to shelter under the cloak of the Son of Autumn, not a part of the Bastard's motley collection of vermin, so Pen was encroaching a trifle on another god's territory, here. More critical was the sheer size of the victim. Killing large animals wasn't just a little like using magic to kill a human would be; it was exactly like it. Knowing not just in theory, but in repeated practice, precisely how easily he could do it was always an uncomfortable piece of self-awareness for Pen to confront.

But only the once, said Des. *Then the white god would seize me back through your target's death.*

You and I both know that's not invariably true. The exceptions in medical sorcery were fraught indeed, and Pen *wished* he only knew them in theory.

Be that as it may. He would set aside all the chickens in the kitchens for Dubro and Maska, and keep the visits to the abattoir and its ambiguities to himself. And not from greed. Breaking a promising young demon that might serve the Temple for generations yet, here at its very outset, would be a huge, if wholly invisible, loss to that future.

Speaking of his other charges, it was past time to go check on them. Pen thanked Jasenik and his now-wary men, made arrangements for tomorrow, collected his horse, and hurried back up to the fort.

PENRIC'S EVENING was brightened by the receipt of a note from Nikys, gingerly handed to him by one of Adelis's clerks. Eager and anxious, he carried it out into the last light of the hospice courtyard and tore it open. It was all benign domestic news, nothing unexpected or worrisome, and his heartbeat slowed to calm as he read it and read it again. Nikys had a nice turn of phrase when describing Florina's infant tricks.

"All's well, then," he muttered to Des. Nikys hadn't added *Wish you were here*, but maybe Pen was wishing that hard enough for both of them.

Yes, observed Des, reading as usual over his shoulder, or through his eyes. *Nothing in it to distract you from your duties, to be sure. It's what good wives do.*

Pen hesitated. *Does it seem too cheerful? Do you think she's leaving out anything?*

Mm, probably. I suppose if anything truly dire occurred, she would ask you for help. But, you know, army widow. Their notions of an emergency are not trivial. She'll be keeping her fears to herself.

Pen wasn't sure whether to be grateful or distressed.

I expect she'd prefer grateful.

"I suppose..." He wanted to be his wife's buttress and confidant, not someone she thought she had to coddle or tiptoe around.

Pen tucked the note in his sash. With luck, he'd get a moment tonight to dash off a reply. He wanted to tell her about Dubro, among other things. He tried not to think too much about his unfinished Cedonian translation of Ruchia's second volume, which he'd left scattered in bits all over his study, in an order understood only by him. He should remind Nikys to restrain Lin from attempting to tidy them up.

Meanwhile, it was time for another pass through the sick-chambers. He'd tightened the interval between rounds by curtailing the prayers to a tap to his lips for his god and the bedside manner to a tap for the magic. The parts he could not reduce were on the other end, the travel between fort and village and town, and the running back and forth from hospice to kitchen to wherever to find poor creatures to kill. He hoped the abattoir would improve his efficiency, if Des could bear the larger loads of disorder between visits.

Urgh, from Des. As a rule demons relished chaos, but she was not enjoying this version any more than he was.

THE NEXT few days and nights blurred together without much distinction, except, while Dubro treated the lesser cases over and over, Pen was able to hit Vilnoc twice a day, Tyno three times, and the worse-off men in the fort sometimes four. Between one visit and the next, and more between one day and the next, Pen could *see* his labors having an effect, not just delaying but pushing back the fever and bruising and pain. It felt like the difference between watching dry mountain grass roots stubbornly survive the winter, and eager bean sprouts break ground in the spring.

The abattoir remained useful and its crew helpful, although after that big-eyed, tame, and unusually friendly calf, which had nudged Pen's hand as if looking for its mother's milk, Pen remembered why he'd gone off eating meat for a while in Martensbridge.

He fantasized about burning his fraying vestments when he finally reached home. The women of the household would likely object to this disposal of their prior labors, wanting at least to make them into kitchen towels or, the last refuge of rags, braided rugs. He hadn't read a letter from his correspondents in other realms or a book, new or old, in…weeks, yes, it had been well over two weeks this had been going on. Was there ever to be an end, or was he to toil on endlessly as if caught in some centuries-long curse from a nursery tale?

His moaning to Rede in the mess, as the one man likely to understand his need to vent his frustrations, produced an unexpected reply.

"Well, of course. Whenever you start to get ahead, you don't rest; you just add in an extra pass. I'm going to start forcibly taking the improving men away from you soon. I can see the difference too, you know. More men are recovering, and recovering faster, since Learned Dubro's arrival allowed you to increase the frequency of treatments. You said that would be so, and so it is."

"The opposite would also be true, you realize, if we get more sick in. How many today?"

Rede's lips stretched in a weird white grin. "Here in the fort? None."

"What?"

"None."

"That…can't be true. It's probably an artifact of chance, and tomorrow we'll get double, or some such." Pen added, as if he were a moneychanger attempting to balance his scales, "There were two more sick in Tyno."

"How many there no longer need your magics?"

"It's so hard to tell when it's safe to stop."

"I see."

But there were no more new cases in the fort the next day, either. Nor the following.

"Are we actually *beating* this thing?" Pen asked Rede, more than rhetorically.

"Maybe? Or it's burning out on its own. Contagions do, sometimes. Well, always, eventually."

"Preferably not because there's no one left alive. Sunder it! It was getting around, now it's not getting around, and *why?*"

Rede shrugged helplessly. "If you find out, tell me."

"You'll be the first to know, I promise."

There were no new cases in the fort the next day, either, nor the next; a much more welcome mystery than the disease's arrival, but still maddeningly obscure. Though for the first time, Pen found himself waking in his cot looking forward to his tasks. It wasn't even that he might anticipate an end; it was that he could see that he was making a difference, that his effort was receiving its due reward of success at last. Most heartening.

...And then Adelis rode back into the fort with thirty wounded, forty deathly ill cavalrymen, and two dozen sick Rusylli.

OVER THE next two days, Penric could see all the progress he, Des, and Dubro and Maska had made slipping through his hands.

The fort hospice was designed to take in the sudden aftermaths of battles, although the sole clash near Vilnoc for over a decade had been at the port with a raiding fleet. With more cots set up, the patient chambers absorbed their new load but only just; by crowding, Rede was still able to assign the wounded and the sick each to their own wards. Not that the former couldn't turn into the latter overnight. The Rusylli were sent back to their camp to be cared for by each other, and Penric had a sharp dispute with the exhausted Adelis as to whether he should go in after them.

It was settled only by the Rusylli themselves, who assembled in a frightened, furious gang to turn Pen back at their gate; this, after having to argue with the greatly augmented Orban guard troop to let him pass within. Pen retreated walking backward up the road shouting instructions in Rusylli for how to send him a message should they change their minds, although he was very much afraid that by the point they did, he'd be unable to break away, the time for today's visit being stolen from Tyno, and Tyno's from the fort. He'd not been able to ride into Vilnoc at all, and his imagination had plenty of material to envision the relapses that must be taking place there, because they were taking place *here.*

Atop it all, the fort was generating new cases again, at first from Adelis's returned cavalry troop and grooms. Either they'd acquired the bruising fever a bit later than some of their comrades, or it took different periods to brew up in different men, or both. Pen was not optimistic enough to believe it would remain limited to that still-too-large pool of men.

On the third morning, Dubro reeled in to report to Penric, "Maska won't come when I call!"

Pen looked them over. Maska cowered within his rider a little like Des in the presence of the Divine, but rather more like a whipped dog hiding under a bed. It was almost the opposite of a demon ascending, for a creature with no other way to retreat or escape. Pen could sympathize.

"Your demon is spent," Pen told him bluntly. "Take the rest of today and tonight off. Tomorrow morning, I'll check him again."

"I could do more," said Dubro, his aged face pinching. "We need to do more!"

"I know, and you can't."

"I could at least help out in the hospice? You know I'm not afraid to get my hands dirty."

Pen nodded with respect, but said, "Rede can get Adelis to conscript him more men for that." At some cost in increased desertions, perhaps. "You need to stop and take care of your demon, which cannot be replaced." Pen would filch a few minutes later to write more begging notes to his chapterhouse for sorcerers, any sorcerers, but he'd done that twice already, and Dubro had been the sole result.

"What about your demon?" Dubro squinted in worry at Pen, although with Maska in this hysterical state, his Sight was unavailable to him. "Is she all right?"

"Over two hundred years old. She has more endurance than I do, and has probably seen worse plagues."

Indeed, murmured Des. *Still not fun.*

"She truly cannot ascend and make off with you? I'd swear she seems powerful enough."

"She could."

At our first acquaintance, yes. But you've been growing more powerful yourself, Pen. So, not such a foregone conclusion as it once was.

Haven't you been growing with me? The proportions should be keeping pace.

Hah.

"But she won't," Pen finished firmly. Collapse from fatigue, maybe; could a demon do that? He didn't want to find out.

Then there was nothing for it but to get back to work, from the sick-chambers to the abattoir and around again, with some side-trips to the kitchen's killing room to pick off the poultry that Dubro would not be getting to today.

That evening, he received a note from Tolga in town. She sounded frustrated and angry, either begging or commanding him to return, though futilely in either case. She went on to detail the progress, or regress, of his worst-off patients, confirming his imaginings.

Pen stuffed the note into his sash, where it burned like a coal.

MASKA WAS somewhat recovered the following morning. Pen gave Dubro a strict ration of a dozen patients to treat, and no more. For Maska's sake it should have been half that, curse it. For the fort's, double. This didn't really buy Pen enough time to visit Tyno, but he went down anyway.

There, not at all to his surprise, he found that some of his patients had backslid, one from the tanner clan into death. Which got Pen shouted at by her weeping husband.

"Why didn't you come back? I thought she was getting better! Why didn't you come back sooner?"

There was nothing to say to this but a useless if true, "I'm sorry."

Pen escaped from the grief and recriminations as swiftly as he could, and stood blinking in the half-deserted village street. The abattoir—he should march up there on his way back to the fort, see what poor innocent beast they'd saved out for him next. And then kill it.

Instead, he found himself turning aside at the village temple.

The Tyno temple was a neat little building just off what passed for the main square. Stone-built, with whitewashed stucco on the outside, its sturdiness hinted that it had been designed and built with the help of the local army engineers. Its six sides supported a concrete dome with a round oculus in its center. The streetside face was devoted to the entryway under a portico. One leaf of the pair of wooden doors was hooked open for the day's petitioners to enter and pray or, with luck, leave offerings.

Penric ducked into the dome's cool shade and made the tally sign. The pavement was mere flagstone, but made interesting with a clever pattern of subtle colors fitted together. The five altar-walls bore the familiar profusion of frescoed images associated with each god, more earnest than artistic. On the central plinth, the holy fire had burned down to coals, aromatic with incense. Pen fed it a fresh stick from the wood-basket in passing.

A couple of villagers rose from their prayer rugs before the Mother of Summer's altar, set them in their stack, and nodded warily at Pen on the way out. Nearly all of Tyno knew who he was by now. It didn't, unfortunately, follow that they trusted him.

Pen considered the Mother's altar for a moment, then cast it his usual apologetic touch to his navel. He turned to the Bastard's altar instead and pulled out a rug, made and donated by some devout village woman, to lay before it. He sank to his knees, then, after a moment, prone, in the pose of utmost supplication, arms outflung. It seemed less piety than exhaustion.

What should he pray for? Forgiveness? Not the white god's specialty. More sorcerers, he supposed. Far more people begged the gods to do something for them than ever offered to do something for the gods, and he wondered if the Five ever grew tired of it. Maybe They were too vast, and so prayers fell like raindrops into the ocean. Pen tried not to bother his god more than he was absolutely forced to, not because he thought the Bastard wouldn't answer him, but because he feared He might, and then what?

He tried to compose his seething mind into a proper mode of holy meditation, open or baiting, he wasn't sure. Slowly, he settled. There seemed more danger that he would simply fall asleep.

Yawning and about to give up, he became aware that Des had shrunk within him to a defensive ball. Deprived of Sight, he extended his ordinary senses to their utmost. Nothing but the musty scratchiness of the rug beneath his cheek, the faint snap and scent of the plinth fire, distant echoes through the door and the oculus from the village life outside.

A tickle on the back of his left hand.

He turned his head to blink owlishly at a horsefly feasting on a drop of blood. The tiny wound did not hurt or itch; could the creature somehow subdue the pain in its victims to give it longer to feed? How, and was it something Pen might learn how to use…?

As horseflies went, it wasn't as big and ugly as some; its body and wings were a pretty iridescent blue.

The connections fell in all at once, like a tower crashing down in an earthquake. *Blood. Rede's flea theory. The blue witch…*

Pen spasmed up, grabbing for the fly, which circled through the air and out the oculus. *Sunder* it.

"Des! Was that accursed thing an *answer to my prayer?*"

I don't know, she gasped. *I couldn't watch.* Slowly, she unfolded again.

Unhelpful, Des!

Pen shouted in frustration to the oculus, "You could stand to be less *obscure*, You know!" He ran outside and looked up, but the fly was long gone. Not that he could see such a speck at this distance anyway.

No matter. Where there was one fly, there were bound to be a thousand more somewhere. If not up at the fort right now. He tried to think if it was of a kind he'd ever seen before. Perhaps not? Certainly not in the cantons, where he'd been enough of an outdoors boy to observe such things. The blue color was very distinctive.

His brain picking at the problem, he walked distractedly back up to the abattoir.

As he trudged past the building to the killing yard, raised voices reached him along with the reek. Jasenik had a good sergeantly bellow. The other's was sharper and more whiny. He rounded the corner to see an overgrown bull-calf waiting in a chute, presumably Pen's current ration, Jasenik, and a groom from the fort holding the lead line of a trembling horse.

"I *told* the cavalry not to send those sick beasts here with my good food animals!" said Jasenik, irate. "Take it straight down to the tanners."

"Well, nobody told me!" complained the groom.

"What's this?" asked Pen, coming up to the group.

Jasenik wheeled. "Ah, Learned Penric. This here's a beast you can kill with my good will. Except not here. Let it walk itself down to the village, if it can."

"What?" said Pen. It looked to be a shaggy steppe pony, normally an incredibly hardy breed.

Not now; its eye and coat were dull, its head hung down, and its legs shook. Blood was crusted around its soft muzzle.

"It has the bloody staggers," the groom informed him glumly. "We've been getting a string of them. We separate them out and put them down in a pasture by themselves as soon as we're sure, and some of them come around again, but this one isn't going to get better."

Des, Sight.

If Penric hadn't been head down for weeks at the closest range to an endless parade of people with the disease, he wasn't sure he could have recognized it in an animal. But he had been and he did, near-instantly.

"That's not the bloody staggers. Well, I'm sure you call it that, in horses. It's this accursed *bruising fever.*"

Both men jerked back. "What?" said Jasenik. "People don't get horse diseases!"

Pen was shaken by a moment of doubt. It was a new idea to him, to be sure. Was it too wild, too desperate?

Des, after a moment, offered, *Thrush. Amberein once treated a poor fellow with a thrush infection in his mouth. Though I doubt he got it from licking the frog of a horse's hoof, so I don't insist on the connection.*

Really…? Pen fought off the distraction; also the repulsive image. "How long ago did you have these sick horses show up at the fort?" he demanded of the groom.

The fellow squinted in thought. "A month ago? No, two? Not more'n two."

Within days of the first outbreak, then. "Where did they come from?"

"Well, this lot"—he jerked his thumb at the trembling horse—"came in with a string of war prizes from Grabyat. But, y'know, any horse seems to get it. And one mule, so far."

"Oxen? Other animals?"

"Not so far as I know. Just horses. The cavalry master is fit to be tied."

"And *nobody* thought to tell Master Orides, or Master Rede?"

The groom stared. "They don't treat horses."

"Brought down the western road from Grabyat?" Past the border town and fort that also reported struggling with an outbreak of the bruising fever? Nothing so likely as for such live battle booty to be set to rest a while at such a fort before being sent on to walk the breadth of a duchy.

"How else? Nobody's going to ship them all the way around the Cedonian Peninsula by sea."

"*Where* do you sequester—keep apart—your sick horses?"

"Up t' road"—the groom pointed upstream—"at the farthest pasture, beyond the woodlot."

"I have to see them." Pen turned, turned again. "Don't give that horse to the tanners. It has to be buried whole and untouched someplace away from people, deep enough the dogs don't get to it. No one should get its blood on them. ...I might be able to get back to kill it bloodlessly for you by the time you round up some men and get a trench dug somewhere."

"What, nobody's going to do that on my say-so!" said the groom, startled by Pen's vehemence.

"Not yours. Tell the cavalry master Learned Penric ordered it." That Penric was nowhere in his chain of command wasn't something to point out just now. "I'll be back later to explain it to Adelis. And everyone. If I can prove what I think is so."

As he turned again toward the road, Des moaned, *Pen, please.*

Oh, right. He waved at the bull calf, which dropped in its tracks. Des sighed relief.

Then he just ran.

PEN STRODE and jogged and didn't stop till he reached the far pasture, which turned out to be a good two miles up the road. He leaned on the gate and caught his breath, studying its occupants. The equine equivalent of the hospice, Pen supposed.

About a dozen disconsolate horses, and one mule, drifted listlessly about, or stood with their heads hanging down but not grazing. One gelding lay on its side, clearly at its last gasp. Pen let himself in and started hunting strange blue flies.

Normal horseflies tended to swarm in their damp breeding places, disgusting enough for anyone encountering them. If one fly was repulsive, dozens of the big buzzing things stooping at you was dozens of times worse. For a few minutes, Pen wondered if he'd flown off the handle about this theory, but then he began to spot the blue intruders, in shy singles clinging quietly to the horses' undersides, or in the inner shadows of their loins. In a few minutes, he'd collected and killed a whole handful. He plucked out fabric in his sash to make a temporary pocket, and tucked them gingerly within.

He then set Des to slaying every fly and parasite of any kind in the pasture, and picked out the least-sick horse there, a black mare that would have been quite comely when well. Pen transferred the biggest blast of uphill magic to the mare that Des could manage. The mare snorted and shied, but thankfully didn't drop of a heart attack; he dumped the chaos into the dying gelding, speeding its demise. Following this up with a strong shamanic compulsion upon the mare to obedience, which he was going to pay for with a nosebleed shortly, Pen shoved her out the gate and scrambled aboard boosted by a foot to the fence. He grabbed mane and kicked her, bridle-and-saddleless, to a canter down the road.

He didn't stop or turn aside at Tyno, though the mare briefly tried to dodge toward the fort; cavalry mount, right. She probably wanted to go home as much as Pen did. He kept her moving at the best pace he could force until they reached the guard post at the Rusylli camp. He was just as out of breath and disheveled as if he had run the whole way, his face and tunic smudged with blood, but at least he'd got here faster. The mare stood puffing, sweating, and trembling as he slid off her bare back, but nudged him and tried to follow as he strode up to the gate guards. Who stepped back in alarm.

"Let me through," Pen snarled, and didn't wait for a reply. A dozen heavily armed soldiers recoiled out of his path.

No unwelcoming committee greeted him this time. Everyone in sight whisked out of it, into the huts or the trees.

Pen, after a frustrated moment, stood in the middle of the clearing and bellowed in Rusylli, "If someone doesn't come out and talk to me *right now*, I'm going to burn every one of your huts to the ground!" He illustrated this empty—probably—threat by setting alight a small, innocuous shrub that straggled nearby. Summer-dry, it went up with a satisfyingly menacing roar. It died down just as fast, but Pen kept an eye out to be sure the conflagration didn't spread.

After a couple of minutes of skittish silence, a familiar figure emerged from one of the huts: Rybi's aunt Yena. Her gray-muzzled hound, whining and cringing as he neared the incendiary Penric, nonetheless faithfully followed, and Pen thought of Maska.

Bravely, Yena straightened her shoulders. "What is it, god man?"

Pen thrust out a hand with a few iridescent dead flies in it, and demanded, "Is *this* the blue witch?"

She drew nearer and peered, then glanced up at his wild-eyed state as if fearing for his sanity, or possibly for anyone in range of his insanity. "I don't know…?"

"Do you know anyone who might? Likely an older woman, or someone from the western clans."

Her lips compressed in thought. "Maybe. Wait here."

She vanished into the grove. Pen jittered in impatience and anxiety.

In a few minutes, *more* minutes, she returned with an even more aged woman. This one was a proper crone, rheumy-eyed and hobbling on a stick, and Pen wondered if she'd been one of the weak ones left behind when the encampment had tried to escape. Adelis had mentioned such, though only to speculate why they hadn't been killed or suicided when their kinsmen fled, a dreadful defiance sometimes practiced among the Rusylli at war.

Pen asked her, "What do the western Rusylli call this kind of horsefly?"

She squinted shortsightedly into his palm, then jerked back and made an averting hex sign, of no actual magical value. "Those evil things! We called them blue witches when I was a girl. Give you a nasty bite. We killed them wherever we saw them."

"Bastard's tears." Pen scrunched his eyes in something like a prayer of gratitude; drew a deep breath. "*Thank* you."

He shoved his sample flies back into his sash and ran for his horse.

PENRIC FOUND Adelis in his map-room-and-scriptorium, sitting at his writing table with his arms folded atop it. The groom from the abattoir and a wiry, leathery-faced man whom Pen recognized as the fort's cavalry master, Captain Suran, stood before him. All three men looked around as Pen panted through the door.

"Well, here's the mage himself," said Adelis. "This should settle the matter." He raised his eyebrows in curiosity at Pen's hectic state. Pen dug half-a-dozen dead blue flies out of his sash and cast them across the table. Adelis leaned back, startled at this abrupt, bizarre gift.

"*Here* are our killers. Or at least the contagion's couriers. These are what the actual western Rusylli dub blue witches."

Adelis frowned in surprise. "Not a sorcerer or a ghost or a demon or a nursery tale? I thought that was what you were thinking."

"I was. I'm fairly sure that's what my first Rusylli informant thought, too. But you know how that goes. One person recounts an observation, the listeners misunderstand, mishear, or just embellish it according to their fancy, and three relays down the line it is changed out of all recognition. Sometimes just one relay."

"How, couriers?" said the cavalry master. "What can horseflies have to do with this bruising curse?"

"Cursed, certainly by me, but not a curse. The fever's not uncanny, however ghastly. The contagion is carried in the blood. Rede guessed it right, though it wasn't rats and their fleas to blame after all. From horse to human, apparently, through the cuts made by these blood-sucking flies. One bit me down in the Tyno temple a while ago."

Pen didn't add his theological speculation about that event.

He held out his left hand in evidence. A trickle of blood still spun over its back, although Pen expected that was mostly a side-cost of his shamanic persuasion upon the mare. It would only confuse his audience to stop and try to explain that right now, and the demonstration was, ahem, handy. Usefully dramatic, supporting the unwelcome news he was going to impart next.

"Mine isn't a guess, Adelis. I went to look at the horses in your cavalry's hospice pasture. I collected these flies there, some from directly off their hides. I could *see* the disease within them. Five gods know, I've been studying it deeply enough in people for the past weeks. Bloody staggers be sundered, it's the same sickness, and why didn't anyone *tell us*...! The infected horses act as blood reservoirs for it. They need to be slain and buried at once. The flies, well, Dubro and I and everyone else can go after them, but we're much more able to *find* the horses. I still don't know if ordinary horseflies or houseflies can also act as blood-couriers, once the sickness is established in an animal, but I doubt anyone will complain if we kill them too." Pen paused for breath.

The groom made a harried gesture at Pen as if to say, *See, there was what I was trying to tell you all!*

The cavalry master had drawn back in repugnance and dismay. "*All* our horses?"

"Gods, I don't know. I hope not. The ones who are far into it, displaying obvious symptoms, you can identify for yourselves. You already have. The ones in the early stages, Learned Dubro and I could likely tag for you, and so spare the clean ones. If we have time." Pen was already *so late* getting back to his next round in the hospice. But, since it was a matter of perception, not the more taxing magical manipulation, maybe he could let the bulk of the task fall on Dubro and Maska? "I don't know yet if horses that appear to have recovered can still act as blood-reservoirs or not."

"If you call for our well-seeming mounts to be taken out and killed, it's going to cause a mutiny among my men." And the cavalry captain looked as though he didn't know which side he'd be on.

Adelis was equally appalled. "Must they be? Can't you heal them as you've been doing for my men?"

"In theory? Maybe. It would have to be tested. But right now, over in the hospice, we're having to choose which *men* to save. If you dump a hundred horses onto my roster as well, I'll be able to save no one." He added in reluctance, "Once all the people, here and in Tyno and Vilnoc, are past the crisis, maybe Dubro and I could try. Something."

"But if you have your way, my horses will be killed by then!" With a gesture at Pen, Captain Suran demanded, "Do you believe this wild tale, General?"

Adelis's hand drifted to touch the burn scars framing his eyes. "Yes," he said heavily. "In matters of his craft, Learned Penric is unequalled in my experience."

Since Adelis's prior experience of sorcerers, Temple or hedge, was almost none, this wasn't as ringing an endorsement as it sounded, but the horse-master nodded unhappily.

"And the Rusylli," Pen added. "I must treat them, too, if they will let me back into their camp."

Adelis looked as though he'd rather put his cavalry horses first, but this time he didn't try to argue. To be fair, the Rusylli were sufficiently horse-mad, they might have agreed with this.

"...Which makes me wonder if the Rusylli encampment will be protected from new cases by its distance, as it seemed to be at the first outbreak. I think the blue flies can't go too far without their horses, or the disease would have traveled east from the steppes long before this." Pen paused, shaken by a horrific notion. Could he himself have carried the disease into Vilnoc, hidden within his borrowed army mount?

It was already there by then, Des chided him. *Calm down, Pen.*

Oh. Right. But that it had traveled somehow from the fort to town, quite possibly in or with a horse or its flies, as it seemed to have hitched its ride from Grabyat, was a logical-enough speculation.

"Were any sick horses or mules taken into town, do you know?" Pen asked.

"Of course not," said the cavalry master, and "Uh…" said the groom.

All three men looked at him. He went mute, frightened.

"Spit it out," Adelis growled, "or it will go badly for you."

The groom gulped. "Maybe…somebody who was told to take a few down to the tanner might have taken them into the town market and sold them, instead? Not me!" he added hastily. "He didn't get much for them, if so."

The market. All sorts of people from all over town might have gone to the market on the dangerous days that the sick horses were present, explaining the random distribution. And, as Pen had just experienced, the bites of the flies were hardly noticeable, and so not recalled a few days later when the first fever symptoms showed. Other horses as well, probably, and oh gods someone was also going to have to trace *those.*

Adelis rubbed his face in uttermost exasperation. He pointed to his cavalry master. "Find out if this is true. If it is, secure the man or men and report back to me."

"Yes, sir," said the daunted Suran.

"Gods, I will hang them," muttered Adelis.

"I'll help," Pen told him through his teeth.

"I thought you weren't allowed to kill."

"By demonic magic. Ropes are not included in that. Executioners are in the white god's flock, come to think. I'll at least give the hangman my learned blessing, if this proves out."

Adelis shook his head. "I do wonder about you some days…" He sat up, gathering himself to issue the necessary, unpleasant orders, and called for his aides.

Before he left the scriptorium, Pen seized quill, paper, and ink to write a hasty note to Nikys, warning her of the newly discovered danger.

...At once devise a covering, cheesecloth or gauze, for Florina's cradle. Fasten it firmly around the edges so no fly can creep through. If the cloth can be found, make tents for everyone's beds as well. In the tighter wooden houses of the cantons, Pen thought a person might stretch and tack cheesecloth across the windows for insect-proof screens, but the open Cedonian-style architecture in Orbas would make this unfeasible. Still. *Tell our neighbors with children this trick.* He thought a moment. *Better, tell them all. Kill any fly you see within the house, but not with your hand. I'll be back as soon*—he scratched this last line through. *I don't know when I will be back. Things are about to get even busier for me here, but we may be able to find our way to the end of this thing at last.*

And then another letter to the medical officer at the border fort, describing Pen's new findings, the blue fly, and his drastic recommendations for containing the contagion. He trusted they'd found themselves their own sorcerer by now to endorse his advice, not to mention carry it out, or it was going to sound like raving. *And*—Pen stifled a moan—someone was going to have to examine the entire track through Orbas that Adelis's cavalry had taken chasing down the Rusylli... He finished with a shorter scrawl to Tolga, who at least required less explanation.

He shoved all three notes into the hands of Adelis's clerk with a demand to dispatch them instantly, and hurried to the hospice.

REDE AND Dubro were coming out of a sick-chamber together when Pen jogged into the hospice courtyard.

"Where have you *been?*" Rede's voice was edged with the sort of anger only fear lent. "We expected you back hours ago!"

Pen danced up to him, grabbed him by the hands, and spun him around. "And time well-spent it was! Rede, I've *cracked* this nut!" Well. In theory. Practice was going to be harder, but wasn't it always?

Rede shook him off and stared at him as though he'd gone mad, which Pen supposed he looked. *Elation* hadn't been anyone's face around here for a while.

Eagerly, Pen dug out his sample flies and repeated his explanations. The two men drew close, ex-farmer

Dubro nodding understanding sooner than Rede did. Hesitantly, Pen added to Dubro, as he had not to Adelis, a fuller description of his and his demon's experience before the Bastard's altar in Tyno.

Dubro's eyes went wide. "Do you think you were god-touched?"

"The Bastard being what He is, I never quite know. But Des reacted the way she does to the Divine, which is to retreat." Cower, to be precise.

No need to be rude, she sniffed.

"And the fly bite"—Pen waved his left hand—"would be typical of His humor."

Rede captured his hand and squinted at the wound, which was finally crusting over, in professional curiosity. Glancing more closely at the bloodstains on Pen's tunic, he frowned. "That's your blood? Not a patient's?"

"Shamanic magics are a whole other discipline, which I will be delighted to describe to you in detail—"

"I daresay," murmured Rede, who was beginning to know him.

"But not right now. First I need to take Dubro—no, first I need to—no, first I need..." Pen paused and took a deep breath, holding it for a moment, then began again. "First I need to take a pass through here and tap my worst-off patients. Then I need to take Dubro to the cavalry stables and show him how to discern the sick horses. This isn't going to make us popular over there, so I have to make sure everyone understands the onus falls on me, not him."

"If anyone complains," said Rede grimly, "take their names. I'll draft them as relief orderlies. That should educate them in a hurry."

Pen nodded agreement, gathering that this wasn't in the least a joke.

"May I treat more patients?" said Dubro. "I think Maska could, now."

"No. Well, maybe. If there is going to be an end to this thing, I may not have to guard your demon's endurance as closely. But separating the sick horses and eradicating the flies comes first for you, because that will stop new cases from coming."

"How soon?" asked Rede, intent.

"Not wholly sure, but I realize now it had already started to happen, before the cavalry came back with all their sick—men and mounts and parasites—and began it all over again." And the Rusylli, never forget them. "I must have killed all the blue flies in the fort along with the others, around when I was first divesting chaos. However long it takes for the disease to brew up in the last man bitten, that will be our end-point."

Until other flies flew in, from whatever pockets they were breeding at—odd corners of Tyno, up and down the river valley, and oh gods, Vilnoc. Infected animals in the village and town were going to be a thornier problem than in the fort, as no one was going to be willing to give up their valuable beasts if they weren't obviously very sick.

General Arisaydia having no direct authority to order such compliance among civilians, Penric would have to call in Duke Jurgo on that problem. Adelis, bless him, had been fielding inquiries from the duke right along, not to mention shielding Pen from demands that he attend on the palace, giving the very just excuse that Pen had been up to his elbows in the sick and shouldn't enter there. If any of the duke's family, retainers, or servants had come down with the bruising fever, Pen had no doubt his priorities would have been abruptly rearranged for him. Persuading Jurgo to support the slaughter out of his purse, *argh* that was not going to please his patron duke; add that to Pen's list of chores. Next-next.

Rede's breath drew sharply in. He grabbed Pen's left hand again and bent to stare at the scab. "Last man bitten. Is that *you?*"

"Uh..." In the excitement of his discovery, Pen hadn't even thought of the disease being included with the holy gift of inspiration. Might the white god have made sure that Pen could not possibly miss the point by sending him an infected fly? Pen was afraid the answer was *Absolutely.*

Be careful what you pray for, sighed Des.

"It's too soon to tell," Pen told Rede and the freshly anxious Dubro. "But in any case, Des can cure me just as we cure others. She once healed me of a fractured skull, and trepanned me for the clot to boot. Of course, the problem was I had to stay *conscious* through it all..."

"Mother's blood," swore Rede. "I want to hear that tale."

"Later," Pen promised. "Best over a gallon of wine. Oh." He turned to Dubro. "This may not have come up in your training, but one sorcerer cannot heal another. Incompatible demons. Before you go home, I must teach Maska some more tricks for keeping you well."

Dubro's eyes were still wide. "Thank you...?"

Pen grinned at both men. Compelled by his momentary euphoria, they smiled back, rare and welcome expressions. “All right. Let’s get to it!”

AFTER HIS pass through the sick-chambers, Pen put the most important tasks in train as quickly as he could. In the cavalry stables, Dubro proved able to sort out the diseased mounts almost as readily as Pen. Leaving Captain Suran to deal with the uproar in their wake, Pen led his colleague down to Tyno for the first time, through orienting visits to his sickest patients, and on to the tannery. Pen was unsure if the heavy outbreak of fever in that clan was from fly bites or the infected blood to which the tanners had been exposed in their work, but then, he was still unsure whether Master Orides might have picked it up from those first autopsies. In any case, they found alien flies in the smelly work-yard. Blue witches, indeed.

Maska dispatched them handily. Evidently, the dog-demon relished hunting deadly blue flies quite as much as hunting rabbits or weasels back in his farm days. So Pen was confidently able to leave the pair to quarter the village and its environs looking for more. Any sick horses or mules would have to be left until someone with more authority could get here, but with the flies gone, they wouldn't be such an immediate hazard.

He circled back via the abattoir, where some sheep that he'd have to greet on his plate tomorrow awaited. Really, he was going off meat. He explained about the imported horses and the invading steppe flies to Sergeant Jasenik and his men; Jasenik was both horrified and smugly validated in his views on sick livestock. In any case, neither sheep nor flies of any description were left alive behind Pen when he slogged up to the fort.

Where, in the westering light of the entry court, a distraught cavalryman attempted to run him through with his lance.

Pen was so tired by now that even with Des's startled aid he almost didn't dodge fast enough. The spearpoint, which the man had been trying to drive into his back, ripped through Pen's tunic and skin and skittered over his ribs under his left arm. The shaft burst into sawdust and the point spun away, a moment too late to spare him the blow.

"Bastard bite it!" Pen swore, turning around and preparing to disable the fellow's legs through his by-now-practiced nerve twist. But a couple of shocked gate guards had run up and tackled the cavalryman for him.

"Oh," wheezed Pen. "Good." He dabbed at the red wet on his side. It would start to really hurt in a minute, he supposed.

"Learned sir! Are you all right?" A passing officer grabbed him anxiously by his arm.

Do I look *all right?* Scarlet was seeping through his torn tunic and down his trouser leg, which would have to be mended and laundered now, blast it. Irritated, Pen shook him off. "Don't get my blood on you. It might be contaminated."

The man recoiled.

"Learned sir!" called a guard holding the struggling would-be assassin. "What should we do with him?" The cavalryman was still swearing at Pen. And weeping. Had they already started the sick-horse slaughter, and with his beloved mount? Evidently.

The cavalryman was quite a young soldier, Pen saw, though past being a boy. Years younger than Pen. As the last in his family, not to mention bearing a centuries-old demon that would make anyone feel a child, Pen still felt awkward with seniority and the duty of care that came with it, for all that it could only become more common in his future.

"Just take him to Captain Suran," Pen sighed. "Tell him what happened. Maybe he can rule it a temporary madness." *Unless it happens again.* Pen hoped not. "I don't have *time* to deal with this."

"Can I escort you to the hospice, sir?" asked the anxious officer.

Pen stared glumly at him. "I know my way by now, I promise you."

Oh, said the outraged Des, still a little frenzied from the sudden attack and defense, *we could be a lot more sarcastic than that! Let me, let me!*

Settle down.

Well, he'd wanted to report in to Master Rede anyway. Pen put his unwashed-since-the-abattoir hands behind his back to keep them there as he continued his trudge to the hospice. He wasn't dizzy. Was he? Not from this shallow if ragged cut…

Rede greeted him with interest and then, as he took in the gory details, horror, and rushed Pen to a treatment room. Pen sat gratefully on a stool and let himself be fussed at, although Des was already stopping the bleeding. *That tunic's done for*, Pen thought as it came off at Rede's hands and landed in a heap.

"Does this hurt?" Rede asked, coming at him with a sponge of wine spirits.

Why did people even *ask* that? "Like a bitch," Pen gasped as the cleansing fluid hit. "It was all right *before* you got your paws on it."

"Aye, I don't think so," said Rede, swabbing grimly as Pen flinched. "Do you *know* you're in shock, Master Not-really-a-physician?"

"Am I?" said Pen doubtfully, and "Yes, you rather are," put in Des aloud.

"I see this in my army idiots. I don't expect it of you."

"Ngh." Pen added after a moment, "I was going to try to ride into Vilnoc tonight."

"And now you're not," said Rede firmly. His hands didn't stop working.

The room was turning. *Then* the nausea hit. Pen countered it with deep breaths.

"Your demon was right when she told the general you wouldn't know when to stop," Rede complained on. Pen didn't argue with him. There were very few people in the fort that poor Rede could vent his feelings upon at the moment, just Pen and, well… Pen. And Des, maybe.

"This is why medicine can't be my calling," said Pen dimly. "The demand is endless, and I've learned I am not. Only the gods could deal with all the world's pain, all at once, all the time. It's a wonder *they're* not driven mad. Unless they have been, which would explain some things. Theologically speaking. Even a sorcerer can't be a god, not all by himself. Although desperate people will try to make him so."

"Nor can a physician," sighed Rede.

"Aye."

THE *ALL by himself* problem was partially addressed for both of them, late the following morning, when a large traveling coach rolled up to the fort gates and disgorged, of all the people Pen had stopped expecting, the senior sorceress-physician from the Mother's Order at Jurgo's winter capital. Along with a crew of her aides.

Learned Master Ravana was a small, aging woman radiating the dense presence within her of a demon at least four generations old. For once, Des had no sly jibes about the rival. Pen had the sense of exquisitely polite bows exchanged between high-level diplomatic enemies being escorted to a negotiating table. In any case, after Pen and Rede came dashing out to welcome them all, Ravana's demoness did not interfere with her rider's determined and efficient introductions.

There followed the fastest tour through the sick-chambers that Pen could arrange, along with a clipped description of all that they had discovered. By Ravana's pertinent questions, she had little trouble understanding events. Then Pen ruthlessly commandeered her and her coach to drive them into Vilnoc where he could toss her to the beleaguered Master Tolga.

Given their many commonalities, Pen thought the two Mother's physicians might get along well. For one thing, Tolga wouldn't start already angry at Ravana as she was at Pen for not coming lately, even though he'd been there and the sorceress never had. Because people were illogical like that. Some days, Pen really preferred demons.

Why, thank you, preened Des.

Hush.

Pen might even be able to set the senior sorceress on *Jurgo*, now wouldn't that be a boon. She'd worked for the duke much longer than Pen had.

Pen tucked himself into a corner of the coach, grateful to be sitting down. "Apologies for sitting so close, Learned." His vague gesture took in their two powerful demons, each studiously ignoring the other like two strange cats.

She waved this away. "It can't be helped." She sat back, her eyes narrowing at him. At them. "So, you are the one Duke Jurgo has told me about. I'm pleased to finally get a chance to meet you, though sorry the occasion is so fraught."

"And I, you." It had been Pen's second summoning, she'd told him earlier, backed by a note from Jurgo himself that had torn her out of her own sticky matrix of responsibilities in order to travel to Vilnoc. That, plus the very real possibility that if the bruising fever should jump to the winter capital, she might well find herself dealing with it there, and she'd wanted to be beforehand. She'd been very frank about that, for which Pen was grateful.

Ravana took this chance to ask a few more shrewd questions about the fever, while the aide who'd accompanied them, herself a physician, listened closely. Pen was just glad for a chance to sit down, though as the coach rocked through a rut, he touched his ribs and winced.

Ravana nodded to his side. "And just what happened there? The wound looks fresh, even with uncanny healing."

Pen was wearing his old house tunic this morning, but she'd recognized his status instantly upon meeting due to his dense demon. His injury was doubtless as bare to her Sight beneath the cloth and bandages as anyone else's would be to him and Des. He sighed and recounted the incident with the murderously upset cavalryman.

Her lips twisted in resigned understanding. "So sad about the horses. But I have to believe you are doing the right thing in removing them as swiftly as possible. Poor young fellow! Will they hang him?"

"I've asked them not to. His captain, though furious, was sympathetic to his plight, so I think they'll listen to me."

"I see." She frowned out the window, tapping her knee, then turned a more considering gaze upon Pen. "So. Your Darthacan translation of Learned Ruchia's two volumes on sorcery came to my hands last year," she went on. "Duke Jurgo kindly sent it over."

That must have been the version printed back in Martensbridge several years ago, which had traveled as far as Pen had; possibly one of the very sets Pen had gifted to his patron. "Ah! You read Darthacan?"

"Not as well as I'd like, and most of my apprentices, less. I understand from Jurgo that you are working on a translation into Cedonian?"

"Oh! Yes." Pen brightened. "The first volume is done and waiting for me to recopy onto the metal printing plates. The second, I am still translating."

"The one on medical sorcery, yes?"

"Yes. It's a much thicker and more complicated volume, and so is taking longer."

"Such a work would be a boon to my apprentices."

"That's my hope. When I was in seminary at Rosehall, the scarcity of texts was a source of much contention. And once, a lurid stabbing. That was what first inspired me to develop the plate-making method. Which I describe in the codicil to the first volume. Although not the part about the stabbing."

"I read that." She sat back and favored him with a peculiar smile. "I want copies for my students. And myself."

"You should be able to extract them from Jurgo. It will be his ducal press producing them, if all goes well."

She nodded firmly. "Pray do not let anyone else run you through before it is finished, Learned Penric."

Accidentally implying they'd be welcome to turn him into a pincushion after? Pen, remembering the state in which he'd left his study, could almost endorse the sentiment. He returned a sheepish grin. "I'll try not, Learned."

Then the coach arrived at the Mother's Order, and all was urgent bustle again. The harried Tolga greeted this relieving force with all the joy Pen had hoped, and even spared a smidgen for him as he detailed the story of the sick horses and the blue flies. It was quickly evident he could leave the women to get on with it, so he begged the loan of a chair and bearers to carry him back to the fort.

It wasn't exactly malingering. The spear cut still throbbed, and he could lie back, close his eyes, and extend Des's range and sensitivity to its maximum to slay a swath through every biting insect along his route through Vilnoc to Tyno. After this was over, he never wanted to kill another domestic animal in his life, but he thought he could cheerfully make this bug-slaughter a routine wherever they traveled. It was a start.

IN FIVE days, new cases trickled down to none. By ten, Pen and Dubro and Rede were able to move the last of the victims from the sick-chambers to the recovery barracks. With fewer deathly ill men to spread the magics upon, they healed faster and faster. This left Pen more chances to circle Tyno, with a similar result. Ravana and Tolga reported a matching course of events from the Mother's Order in Vilnoc.

In the middle of all this the Rusylli encampment *finally* sent for his help, and he took Dubro along, not solely in case of more angry spears. To his bemusement, the sick Rusylli responded to the older sorcerer, who spoke not a word of their language, with more trust than they gave the more powerful but younger-looking Penric—Pen was reminded of his obstreperous patients in the fort who had yielded to that same grandfatherly air. It would have been better, always better, if they'd been able to start the treatments earlier, but with the source of new infections cut off, they at least stood a chance of catching up, and within two days Pen was able to leave the Rusylli to Dubro as his special charge.

This also gave him ten days to be very, very sure Des had managed to clear the disease from his own body, because, yes, of *course* that horsefly in the Tyno temple had been infected. Pen wasn't even surprised when his fever began. But since soldiers persisted in eating, no doubt to the dismay of the army ledger-keepers, there was a never-ending parade of beasts in the abattoir to divest chaos upon. Pen added his own body's incipient disorder to the discharge, and his ailment passed off with no other symptoms.

Thirty-six days after he had left home for a two-hour visit to the fort, Pen stood before his own front door once more.

Had the cheerful red-orange paint been peeling this much before? Pen had barely time to wonder if he should get someone on that before it was flung open and Nikys bolted into his arms.

"Oh, you're back, you're well, you're alive, you're *here!*" she cried in excitement, pulling him into the atrium.

Pen let himself be hauled, helpless against his spreading grin, and her. "Hey, hey, I sent you a note yesterday, it shouldn't be a surprise..."

"We've been watching out for you all morning. I promise you, I didn't let Lin touch your study."

"It doesn't matter. I can't remember what I was last doing there anyway," he assured her. For all that he wanted to cling to his writing table like a barnacle and never be scraped off again.

"You've grown so thin!" She unhanded him just enough to scowl down the length of his body. "You could hardly afford that. Des, didn't you make him eat?"

"Army food and general madness," Des defended herself. "Not my fault."

"Well, you'll find neither here."

"Five gods be praised," Pen told her. Footsteps and a faint mew drew his attention beyond her, where Idrene stood holding Florina and smiling. "Oh my word. Her head's grown so much!"

"They do that, about the fourth month," said Idrene placidly.

"Well, yes, I knew that, or Des did—six of her prior riders had been mothers, did I ever say? Before they contracted a demon, of course." His reach toward the sleepy infant was briefly thwarted by Idrene stepping back. "No, I'm clean, I wouldn't be back here if I weren't."

He pried his child away from her and fixed her on his shoulder, stroking the fuzzy head in wonder.

"It's just...marvelous. To marvel at. You are a marvel, yes you are..." He was fairly sure his expression was completely foolish. He was fairly sure he didn't care.

His glance around the atrium found it all... exactly the same, clean and serene, and when had that become a miracle? He spared an arm to snag Nikys. "I have so much to tell you."

She choked on a laugh. "I have so little!"

"No...no...everything here is marvelous." He breathed in her curls. "*Everything.*"

Epilogue

"SO," SAID REDE, fingering the metal rectangle. "This is what a magically finished printing plate looks like."

"You can pick it up," Pen said cordially. "It won't break."

Endlessly curious, Rede separated it from its stack and did so, tilting it this way and that in the bright light from Penric's study window.

"That's still the Cedonian translation of Volume One, which I'm well along with, but I broke off to add a chapter on the bruising fever to Volume Two," Pen told him. "I will be very pleased to have you read the first draft and check it for accuracy, as there's scarcely anyone with more expertise on that subject right now than you, hard-won as it was."

"You," Rede pointed out. "And Master Tolga and Learned Ravana."

Pen nodded concession. "But you're here. Anyway, my plan is to first make it a separate little chapbook, for the palace printer to send around to the relevant Orders in Orbas. Because it seems more locally urgent."

Rede said wistfully, "Do you think all the blue flies have really been eradicated?"

Pen grimaced. "I've been murdering ordinary flies for years, and haven't made a dent in their legions yet. More to the point, wherever the evil things came from, out there among the western Rusylli tribes, they're likely still there. As long as the western Rusylli press on the eastern, and the eastern on the borders of Cedonia, Grabyat, and countries south, they're bound to turn up again."

"Let's pray not for a long time," sighed Rede. Pen vented an agreeing hum, more in hope than belief.

The sounds of Lin admitting a visitor drifted up from the atrium and through Pen's study door, open to catch whatever draft might relieve the heat of this early autumn day. "It's important," said Pen, "but not actually what I invited you here to talk about today. And here's my other guest."

Pen rose to greet Learned Dubro as Lin ushered him into the study. Dubro looked around with great interest. "Ha. This looks a proper scholar's lair."

Pen grinned. "I'd apologize for the mess, but I'm not in the least sorry. Here, sit, sit." Pen cleared a chair of scrolls and pulled it close to Rede's.

The two men exchanged what Pen was fairly sure were mockeries of military salutes. "Good to see you again," said Rede, and, "You as well," said Dubro. There followed a short, social delay while Lin brought in a pitcher of cooled tea and a plate of spiral cakes, curled around spices. Dubro seemed to find their delicacy somewhat alarming, and sat more carefully on his chair as he consumed them.

"So." Pen took a swallow of tea and cleared his throat. "I've been thinking about this for some time. And I've concluded that Master Rede would be an ideal candidate to receive Learned Dubro's demon, upon his passing, and so become Orbas's next sorcerer-physician."

Rede made a taken-aback sound.

Dubro seemed less discomfited. "Don't look like that, young fellow. We all have to go sometime. And

I'd be pleased to know I was leaving Maska in such good hands."

"But—you'd have to die."

"That's the way it works, aye. There's more than one reason the Quadrenes call us Temple sorcerers necromancers. I wouldn't volunteer to leave early, mind you."

"You and I"—Pen nodded to Dubro—"both acquired our demons by accident, if not necessarily by mistake. Receiving one in a planned fashion doubtless feels a much stranger event when the donor-sorcerer isn't a stranger." Pen turned to Rede. "Because it wouldn't just be Maska you'd be receiving. In effect, if the transfer was successful, your head would be haunted for the rest of your life by an image indistinguishable from Dubro's ghost. And human images *talk* to you."

"Maska communicates," Dubro objected. "In his own fashion."

Pen waved allowance.

"It wouldn't be his sundered soul?" asked Rede uneasily. "Cut off from his god?"

"No, not normally. Although in certain botched transfers—well, that goes into technicalities that need not delay us here. Plenty of time to learn about it all later. I've never liked the term *image* for the shape a demon takes from its rider's life, because that would seem to imply something static. Within you, the demon still lives and grows and learns and changes, and will bear all those memories to its next rider. After a few transfers, a demon becomes something of a layer cake. Underneath the ten women who make up Des, that first wild mare and the lioness that killed her still linger. They send me odd dreams now and then."

Dubro nodded. "I get little fragments from the weasel and the quail, sometimes, though Maska looms larger. Dog dreams aren't very colorful, but they smell amazing." Dubro's lips twisted. "I've no idea what Dubro-dreams would be like, though I wouldn't wish some of mine on anyone else. I suppose you'd end up knowing more about me than my wife or mother ever did. But so would whoever inherited my demon. Maybe once your soul is gone to your god, you don't care about embarrassment."

"I think, at that point, the donor-souls have a vaster and stranger world to absorb them," Penric agreed. "The recipient does have to get over the shock of the intimacy." Des snickered. He asked her dryly, *Anything to add from your position of expertise, here?*

No, carry on, she said. *You're doing fine so far. But—layer cake, really?*

I could come up with less appealing metaphors, but I'm trying to sell the idea, here.

Merchant of demons? Peddling demon-flavored cakes, ah, I see.

Stop. You'll make me laugh, and then poor Rede will be even more confused.

She settled back to watching smugly.

"You have a while to think about it," Pen told Rede. "Maybe years."

Dubro eyed his knobby hands, dusted with age spots. "Or maybe not, eh?"

Pen tilted his head in acknowledgement. "Today would be merely a declaration of intent, a preliminary contract."

"Like some peculiar sort of betrothal?" said Rede, which made Dubro, lifting a cake to his lips, snort a laugh, then cough on crumbs. He restored himself with a gulp of tea.

You have no idea, thought Pen. "More a betrothal on one side, a will on the other. But chances happen. It may be that some other Temple demon becomes available first. Or that this one might be lost, Bastard forbid. Although…the white god is the god of chances, good and ill. If He approves, He has unexpected ways of helping make things occur." Pen surreptitiously rubbed the back of his left hand. "Sometimes very subtle." And sometimes less so.

"There would be a spate of required theological study," Pen went on, "which I doubt intimidates you. And Temple oaths, which cap all others. Including military ones, but if you undertake to go on as an army physician, there won't be any trouble negotiating that. You're already adept at balancing your oath to the Mother and your oath to Orbas. You really do have a calling in Her craft."

"This seems a very direct solution to the shortage of sorcerer-physicians that I was complaining about," Rede said ruefully.

"The only one I know of," said Pen. "With the white god, you learn to be careful what you pray for."

Rede puffed a laugh. "So it seems." He set down his tea, took a breath, turned to Dubro, and extended his hand. "Well, Learned Dubro. If it chances so, then, I would like to try this."

Dubro's seamed face curved in a smile as he gripped back. "Master Rede. White god willing, so should I."

The memory of a moment on a spring roadside in the cantons drifted through Pen's mind, curiously doubled. *Let me serve you in your need*, and, *Accepted.* He'd had much less notion than Rede what a wide new world he'd been getting into, back then.

You didn't, no, Des agreed. *I had much less than I thought. But One other guarded us both, I think.*

And we've done all right so far, haven't we, Des?

Aye.

"White god willing," Pen prayed sincerely.